Risky Assignment

Cedar River Daydreams

Live! From Brentwood High

Other Books by Judy Baer

Risky Assignment

JUDY BAER

Risky Assignment
Judy Baer

Cover illustration by Joe Nordstrom

All scripture quotations, unless indicated, are taken from the HOLY BIBLE, NEW INTERNATIONAL VERSION®. Copyright © 1973, 1978, 1984 by International Bible Society. Used by permission of Zondervan Publishing House. All rights reserved. The "NIV" and "New International Version" trademarks are registered in the United States Patent and Trademark Office by International Bible Society. Use of either trademark requires the permission of International Bible Society.

Library of Congress Catalog Card Number 93–74537

ISBN 1–55661–386–5

Published by Bethany House Publishers
A Ministry of Bethany Fellowship, Inc.
11300 Hampshire Avenue South
Minneapolis, Minnesota 55438

Printed in the United States of America

To
Jan G.

Thanks for your enthusiasm

JUDY BAER received a B.A. in English and Education from Concordia College in Moorhead, Minnesota. She has had over thirty novels published and is a member of the National Romance Writers of America, the Society of Children's Book Writers, and the National Federation of Press Women.

Two of her novels, *Adrienne* and *Paige*, have been prizewinning bestsellers in the Bethany House SPRINGFLOWER SERIES (for girls 12–15). Both books have been awarded first place for juvenile fiction in the National Federation of Press Women's communications contest.

Prologue

As flames fiercely licked the sky, a tree toppled to the ground and sparks fell around it like golden rain. The roar of fire and wind echoed in the night skies like the rumble of phantom freight trains. Fire was everywhere, greedily consuming everything in its path.

A lone figure silhouetted against the flames raised a microphone to her lips. "And that's tonight's Channel 9 News. Tune in tomorrow for more on the fire which threatens several homes on the outskirts of Brentwood. Arson, according to Fire Chief Bert McCall, cannot be ruled out. . . ."

Darby Ellison stared at the television screen long after the news had faded to commercial, her chin propped in the palm of her hand, her dark eyes fixed intently on the dancing raisins that had replaced Anna Leemon, Channel 9's top investigative reporter. Darby tried to imagine what it must be like to stand with such awesome wind and fire at one's back—and with the eyes of the entire region watching.

"Are you still glued to the TV?" Ace interrupted her train of thought. With the flick of his wrist, he turned off the television. "You'll get bug-eyed watching it all the time. Pretty soon your eyes will pop out of your head. You'll have to lay your eyeballs on your shoulders in order to see where you're going. It's not going to be a pretty sight, Darb, I'm warning you."

Darby's brother teased her unmercifully when he came home from college. It was the very thing she missed when he was away.

"You aren't a pretty sight either, Ace."

Adam "Ace" Ellison sank onto the couch beside his sister. "You're the only person I know who could watch the news twenty-four hours a day and never get bored."

You just don't get it, do you, Ace?

But, then again, no one did. Not one person Darby knew understood her fascination with either the news or Anna Leemon. But it really didn't matter. It was enough to know that when Anna Leemon decided it was time to leave Channel 9, there would be someone waiting in the wings, ready to take her spot.

And that "someone" is me!

"Did you say something, sis?" Ace looked up from the sports magazine he was skimming.

"Hand me the remote control. There's a show I want to watch."

Ace sighed and, without another word, turned the television to the channel where Darby's favorite anchor was just beginning to read the national news.

ATTENTION JUNIORS AND SENIORS
OF BRENTWOOD HIGH:

OPENINGS AVAILABLE
IN A NEW PROGRAM SPONSORED BY
BRENTWOOD HIGH SCHOOL
IN COOPERATION WITH
LOCAL TELEVISION AND RADIO STATIONS
AND THE BRENTWOOD GAZETTE.

INTERESTED IN DISCOVERING IF YOU HAVE
WHAT IT TAKES
TO MAKE IT IN BROADCASTING?

WANT A CHALLENGE
YOU'LL REMEMBER FOR A LIFETIME
(AND TWO HIGH SCHOOL CREDITS AS WELL)?

CONTACT MS. ROSEMARY WRIGHT IN THE
COMMUNICATIONS DEPARTMENT BY
FRIDAY, SEPTEMBER 12.

ONLY SERIOUS INQUIRIES CONSIDERED.

MS. ROSEMARY WRIGHT
OFFICE #3
HOURS: 2:00–4:30 M–W–F

"Are we ready?" Jake Saunders' fist was curled and poised to knock, knuckles grazing the wooden door. He glanced at the pair standing behind him.

Darby Ellison smoothed the front of her jacket and swallowed. "Ready as we'll ever be. Right, Izzy?"

"Huh?" Eugene Isador Mooney stuffed the last of a candy bar into his mouth, crumpled the wrapper into a wad and jammed it into his pocket.

"Izzy! Pay attention! This is important."

"So knock. What's the big deal? We'll never get an interview from out here."

Jake rolled his eyes and brought his knuckles down hard on the door.

"Hang on. I'll be there in a minute." The feminine voice inside the house was muffled and faint. Momentarily the door swung open to reveal a petite woman with long, dark hair, saucerlike blue eyes, and a huge stomach.

"Mrs. Oakland?"

"You must be the students from Brentwood High. Come inside." She invited them into a large but cozy room with high-beamed ceilings and warm wood paneling. "Walk this way." The woman duck-walked toward a seating arrangement of couches and chairs.

"Don't take me literally, of course. I've almost forgotten *how* to walk. All I do these days is waddle." She patted her rotund belly. "I hope this baby is born soon. I'm tired of looking and feeling like a beached whale."

Darby put her hand over her mouth to cover a smile. Jake and Izzy both looked a little nonplussed by the woman's frankness. It became increasingly clear why Ms. Wright had recommended that the threesome interview Janie Oakland for their news story. Mrs. Oakland wouldn't hesitate for a moment to speak what was on her mind.

She lurched into a chair and put her feet on a small footstool. "Ahh. There. Now I'm ready. What did you say your names were?"

"I'm Darby Ellison, and these are my friends Izzy Mooney and Jake Saunders. We're part of the *Live! From Brentwood High* program."

"Rosie Wright's media class," Mrs. Oakland concluded with a smile. "So you're the kids who are going to put together a feature story every week for Channel 9. Impressive. I'm surprised the news director agreed to give you the time."

"It's a pilot program," Darby said, "and we only get ninety seconds on the air, but it's still a great opportunity. Besides the air time on Channel 9, we do a thirty-minute weekly news show which is shown at school. One of the places it runs is the cafeteria. Some parts of the show are live, others taped."

"Yeah," Izzy added, "and we also have a radio program that is produced and broadcast Monday through Thursday in the cafeteria and select study halls. The challenge is to make it interesting enough to get people to stop talking and start listening." Izzy grinned gleefully. "Some of the commentaries should get pretty controversial!"

"Don't forget the newspaper," Jake added. "That's part of our program too. We do a column once a week which runs in the Brentwood *Gazette*. It's called 'TeenSpeak.'"

"Leave it to Rosie to sniff out opportunities."

Mrs. Oakland chuckled at the startled expressions on her visitors' faces. "Rosie and I attended college together and planned the ways in which we'd change the world, all sorts of idealistic things. And here we are, only thirty miles apart—Rosie's in the city, teaching communications to high-school students, and I'm in the country, growing into a creature the shape of a large beach ball."

Izzy stood gawking at Mrs. Oakland. His mouth was hanging open and his eyes looked a bit glazed. He'd either overdosed on Milky Ways on the drive out or he just couldn't quite figure out the energetic little woman they'd come to interview. Darby nudged him and with her index finger tried to push Izzy's jaw shut.

"It's really nice of you to agree to talk to us." Jake flipped open his notebook and poised a pen over the paper. "Since this is our first story, we have to warn you that we might not be very good at conducting an interview."

"Don't worry. I'm so excited about the EMT— emergency medical technician—program here in Braddington that I'll probably answer questions you don't even *want* to ask.

"It's very difficult to provide adequate medical service to small rural communities," Mrs. Oakland contin-

ued. "Our ambulance service and the EMTs who staff
it save lives. It is an honor to have been the first coordinator of emergency care in this community."

"But you don't hold that position now?" Izzy found
a pen in the pocket of his jacket and began taking notes
on the back of the candy bar wrapper he'd rescued from
his pocket.

"No. I resigned my position when I learned I was
pregnant. I wanted to continue to teach at the high
school and I simply couldn't juggle any more responsibilities. I *am* proud to say, however, that one of my
students—Grady O'Brien—recently completed EMT
training. He's on call several nights a month and, I've
gathered, doing a terrific job."

"How old is this Grady?" Izzy asked.

"Just about your age."

Mrs. Oakland studied the trio as they scribbled
down the information she was giving them. "Why don't
you tell me a little about yourselves before we continue? Rosie didn't give me all the details about your
program."

"It's basically teens producing stories about other
teenagers and the issues that concern them—a news
show *for* teens and *by* teens," Jake explained. "Like we
said, our program, *Live! From Brentwood High*, pro-
vides experience in all aspects of television broadcasting, both behind and in front of the camera as well as
radio and print mediums. We're trying to learn all we
can about mass communications. I—" Jake stopped
midsentence as a grimace of pain contorted Mrs. Oakland's features. "Are you okay?"

"Fine, I . . . oh!" Mrs. Oakland's face was pale.

"Could we get you something?" Darby asked. "Water?"

"No, it's okay. Just these crazy pains."

"Pains?" Izzy echoed, looking alarmed. His gaze rested on Mrs. Oakland's very round stomach. "What *kind* of pains?"

"False labor. I've been having them all day."

"Aren't 'labor pains' what you get before you have a baby? Are you . . ."

"Having a baby?" Mrs. Oakland chuckled. "Of course I am, but not today. According to the medical books I've read, false labor pains are irregular and improve with exercise. I've had these pains before. I even went to the hospital last week. They sent me home again. Apparently false labor is quite common for a first baby. Don't worry. I'm sure I'll know when I'm in real labor." She arranged her hands on the shelf of her stomach. "Now then, where were we?"

It took Jake a moment to gather his composure. He eyed Mrs. Oakland warily as he continued. "Our advisor, Ms. Wright, told us that you'd agreed to talk to us because you were so closely involved with the formation of the rural EMT program. She indicated that because of you, several Braddington High students enrolled in the training program."

"True. And those kids have been real lifesavers, both literally and figuratively. Our ambulance program had been in trouble for several years. It's always been difficult to find volunteers to take the training and make the commitment to be on call nights, weekends, whenever. Most of these students are interested in the medical field. Through the EMT program they are getting some invaluable hands-on training and experience and . . . oh!" Mrs. Oakland's eyes grew wide. "Another one."

"Another *what*?" Izzy asked unsteadily.

"Another pain. Funny," she massaged her belly thoughtfully, "they've never been this close before."

"Maybe you'd like to go to the doctor again?" Izzy asked hopefully.

"That's not necessary. First babies take a long time to come. I have an appointment tomorrow. I'll ask him about it then."

Izzy looked anxiously from Darby to Jake. His round face crumpled with concern. "Maybe we'd better come back another day."

"Nonsense. Besides, I promised Rosie . . . Ms. Wright . . . that I'd arrange a meeting for you with Grady O'Brien. He's the one you'll want to talk to about your story. He's done with his training and has been taking calls for over three months now . . ." Mrs. Oakland's statement trailed away in a whisper.

She cleared her throat and looked at Jake. "You don't happen to have a watch with a second hand, do you?"

"Sure, but . . ."

"Time something for me, will you?"

The authority in Mrs. Oakland's voice suggested that she'd been a teacher for a long time. Obediently Jake raised his wrist and stared at the face of the watch.

"Starting now." There was a sharp edge to Mrs. Oakland's voice.

"How long was that?" A bead of sweat broke out on Mrs. Oakland's upper lip.

"Just under two minutes." Jake's gray-green eyes

were troubled and he looked pale beneath the golden bronze of his not-yet-faded summer tan. His easy, appealing grin had vanished.

Darby felt as if she'd held her breath for the entire two minutes.

"Again. Time it now!" Mrs. Oakland stiffened and totally tuned them out. Whatever was going on now was between her and the second hand on Jake's watch.

"Okay." She breathed deeply and relaxed once again into the chair. "How long?"

"A minute and a half." Jake frowned.

The woman took two deep breaths and rubbed the gently rounded ridge of her stomach. "I think I might be having the baby—now!"

CHAPTER 2

LIVE

FROM DRENTWOOD HIGH

"Whoa!" Izzy leaped to his feet and put his hands on top of his head. His grown-out buzz made him look as though he were caressing a fright wig. "You can't do that!"

A wisp of a smile flitted across Mrs. Oakland's lips. "And who's going to try and stop me? You?"

"Oh, yeah." Izzy stared at the woman in dismay. "Should we call your husband or the doctor?" His question was interrupted by another of Mrs. Oakland's soft moans.

"Ninety seconds again," Jake murmured as he stared at his watch in horror. "The pains *are* getting closer."

"There's a number by the phone," Mrs. Oakland panted. "I don't think my husband will have time to get home for this event. You'd better call an ambulance. Oh, my!"

"Mrs. Oakland?" Darby leaned in close. "What happened?"

"It's for sure now. This baby is on the way. I believe my water just broke."

"Wa . . . wa . . . wa . . ." Darby stammered.

"Water. The sac of fluid that insulates and protects

the baby. It's supposed to break just before the baby is born."

Once a teacher, always a teacher, Darby supposed. Even now, Mrs. Oakland couldn't resist the temptation for an educational experience. She turned calmly to Darby. "Could you hand me that quilt on the back of the couch, dear? I'm a little chilled."

Izzy stumbled backward toward the phone, knocking over a small table and a green plant as he went. A sheen of sweat glistened on his forehead. "Don't do anything till they get here," he pleaded. "Don't have the baby now. I get sick at the sight of blood. I practically flunked biology because I couldn't dissect that frog. . . ."

As Mrs. Oakland began the controlled breathing that helped her through her contractions, Izzy huffed and panted along with her.

Jake wrenched the telephone receiver out of his hulking friend's hand. "Pull yourself together, Izzy." He punched the phone's buttons. "Hello? Braddington Hospital? We need an ambulance at the Oakland residence on Parson's Road. The baby is coming. Do you need directions? No? Okay. Hurry. *Please!*

"They're coming." He turned to the woman in the chair. She suddenly seemed tiny and vulnerable. "What can we do?"

"I suppose we should call my husband. Other than that . . ."

While Jake dialed the phone again, Darby tucked the quilt closer to Mrs. Oakland and then stood aside, helplessly wringing her hands.

"Don't look so frightened," Mrs. Oakland joked weakly. "Look at this as a possibility. You're going to see the Braddington ambulance squad in action."

"She's right!" Izzy bellowed, suddenly revived. "What an opportunity!"

"You don't have to look so happy about it," Darby scolded.

"I wish I'd brought my video camera. I could have taped the whole thing. My first chance at a really interesting documentary and I blew it." Izzy knocked himself in the forehead with the heel of his hand.

"I thought you wanted to make documentaries for public television about how reptiles eat and how monkeys scratch," Jake growled, referring to why Izzy had applied for the program in the first place.

"This is better. A real-life docu-drama. Man, I can't believe I don't have my cam."

Jake rolled his eyes. "For a smart guy, you're a real dope. This is no time to be thinking about the Brentwood program."

"It's okay," Mrs. Oakland assured them. Her breath was coming faster now and she'd broken out in a sweat. "I'd love to have students who are so enthusiastic."

She drew a sharp breath, and for the first time Darby saw fear on Mrs. Oakland's features. Impulsively Darby knelt down and took her hand. "What can I do?"

"Talk. Take my mind off the pain until the ambulance comes."

"About what?" Darby's mouth felt dry.

"Anything. School. The *Live! From Brentwood High* program. Anything!"

"Ah . . . ah . . ." Darby searched her brain for words. "We had our first *Live! From Brentwood High* organizational meeting just last week . . ." she stammered. "Are you *sure* you're all right?"

A single word edged through gritted teeth. *"Talk!"*

Casting a panicked look in Jake's direction, Darby complied. "It's really a great program. High tech. I think I'm lucky to have been chosen. It's like a dream come true." Darby warmed to her subject. "Ever since I was a little kid I've wanted to be on television. First I was going to have my own show for children. Then I wanted to be the weather lady. And for the past few years . . ."

" . . . she's been eyeing Joan Lunden's job on *Good Morning America*." Izzy rested a big, comforting paw on Darby's shoulder. She leaned into his strength, glad he was there.

"Have you two known each other long?" Mrs. Oakland struggled to remain calm as the pains crested and then flowed away in a rhythm old as time.

"Forever."

"Practically. We went to kindergarten together."

"We wouldn't have survived the sixth-grade hygiene lecture and eighth-grade math without each other." Darby eyed the large, lumbering boy with a smile.

For as long as Darby had known him, Izzy had never quite seemed to fit into his own body. It was as though somewhere along the line he'd outgrown his own skin. Even today Izzy's clothing didn't match. Izzy insisted he was color-blind, but more likely, he'd chosen his attire by which items of apparel were lying at the top of the nearest laundry basket.

With Izzy, appearances were deceiving. Under that dreadful buzz cut was the brain of a genius. It had surprised everyone—including Izzy—when testing had proved that there was a potential scholar in the Mooney family. Ever since, both teachers and parents, much to Izzy's dismay, had been trying to make him live up to his potential.

"And you?" Mrs. Oakland's gaze rested on Jake as he joined the others on the floor near her chair.

He looked up at her with those incredible gray-green eyes through smokey eyelashes that went on forever. Darby adjusted for the little flip-flop she experienced in her stomach every time she saw Jake's easy, lopsided grin.

"I'm Izzy's chemistry partner. I met Darby for the first time last week."

"Poor guy," Darby interjected, giving Jake a sympathetic look. "I heard that everyone requested to be switched into another section when they heard Izzy was going to be in the class."

"Hah! What is it with everybody, anyway? What's the big deal about chemistry?"

"You should know better than anyone. You started the fire in the lab last year. We had to evacuate the building."

"That was nothing. Just a little experiment I was conducting. I had a minor problem. That was all."

"It was a three-alarm fire," Jake reminded Izzy. "There were fire trucks everywhere."

"And you weren't even supposed to be in the lab," Darby added. "You hadn't signed up for chemistry. I thought for sure you'd be expelled for that one."

"Why? Nothing happened."

"Nothing but setting the school on fire!"

"A few charred drapes. There's a difference."

"Now the chemistry teacher looks at Izzy like *he* might ignite!" Jake said with a laugh.

Izzy looked injured. "Teachers *like* students who take initiative and do things on their own, don't they, Mrs. Oakland?"

"Izzy, you sound like a wonderful—Oh!" Pain flickered on her features. "The pains are getting stronger. How long until the ambulance arrives?"

"It's only been a couple minutes," Jake glanced at his watch. "It just *seems* like hours."

"Keep talking." Mrs. Oakland took a deep breath and exhaled slowly. "Keep my mind off this pain. Tell me about the others in this program. Tell me about my friend Rosie."

"The first time we saw Ms. Wright she calmly walked to the front of the room and hoisted herself onto her desk. She was wearing bright, crazy clothes and looked at us as if we'd just landed from outer space."

"That's how we looked at her too," Izzy reminded Darby.

"I'm Rosemary Wright, advisor and coordinator for this new program." Izzy did a surprisingly good imitation of Ms. Wright. "I'd like to tell you that the format for this internship is cut, dried, and etched in stone, but I can't. We've never tried anything quite like this at Brentwood before, and we'll be writing the rule book as we go along . . ."

"She's really excited about the ninety-second time slot on the local affiliate station on Saturday nights at the end of the news," Darby interjected. "According to Ms. Wright, ninety seconds sounds short and easy, but it's not. The full story will run on *Live!* and will be edited to ninety seconds for the station's showing. She said we should plan to learn everything we can about a subject, even though it may not appear in the segment."

"Tell me about some of your classmates. What kind of students are interested in this sort of thing?"

Darby spoke the first name that came to mind. "Andrew Tremaine."

"Why'd you start with that geek?" Izzy groaned. "Don't tell her about *him*. You might scare the baby."

Mrs. Oakland reached to clutch Darby's hand. "Tell me . . ." she panted. "Keep talking."

Izzy swallowed thickly. "Talk, Darby. Don't let her have the baby now! Keep her occupied till the ambulance comes."

"As if she could stop a baby from being born!" Jake growled.

"Should we be boiling water or something?" Izzy wondered aloud. "They always do that on *Gunsmoke* reruns. And they tear up old sheets. Do you have any sheets you want ripped up, Mrs. Oakland?"

Darby kicked Izzy in the shin and began to speak. "Andrew is . . . difficult. He thinks he's awfully smart."

"He thinks he's a gift to women," Izzy clarified.

"And *is* he?"

Darby could see a faint smile on Mrs. Oakland's pale face.

"I guess some girls like his type," Darby answered thoughtfully. "He'd be a lot *more* appealing if he didn't know how good-looking he is."

"You think Drew is good-looking? What's he got that I haven't?" Izzy demanded.

"He's six foot two, has dark hair and blue eyes that

look like the ocean. He could model if he wanted to, I think."

"I'm *over* six foot two," Izzy pointed out.

"And your hair looks like a dandelion that's gone to seed," Jake finished. "Besides, your eyes don't match."

"They do too. One is just a little more brown than the other, that's all. It's a Mooney family trait."

Mrs. Oakland moaned a little. Darby looked anxiously toward the window. Where was that ambulance?

"Julie Osborn is also in the program," Darby rushed on. "She wants to be an anchorperson on the national news."

Izzy made a derisive sound at the back of his throat. "That's like hoping a political science class will make you President of the United States. Of course, Julie's the most stuck-up person in my English class. She'd probably run for queen if we had one."

"Don't forget Kate Akima," Jake added.

"I don't know her very well," Darby admitted. "I met her for the first time at the organizational meeting of *Live! From Brentwood High*. She's very attractive." Kate had short, silky black hair cut into a bob which gently skimmed her jaw.

"What about Shane Donahue?"

Darby recalled the jolt she'd felt when she'd discovered that Shane was going to be a part of *Live! From Brentwood High*. Shane's reputation around Brentwood was far from exemplary. Restless, brooding, and always on the fringes of trouble, Shane was one of Brentwood's "bad boys."

She felt a blush creep up her neck and across her cheeks. She'd had a crush on Shane once. Fortunately he'd never found out, and she'd come to her senses in time. Shane was as careless with the girls in his life as he was with his reputation.

She was grateful when Izzy suggested another name. "Joshua Willis is in the program too."

"He's a great guy," Jake commented.

Josh, a slender African-American with a gentle voice and sweet smile, had impressed them all.

"Keep going," Mrs. Oakland said through gritted teeth.

"I can't believe Molly Ashton applied," Izzy said, oblivious to Mrs. Oakland's discomfort. "What an airhead! She used to date Blake Denton. They just broke up a couple of weeks ago. Blake's got a new girl, but Molly is still moping around. She should get a life!"

"She's not so bad," Jake protested. "I like her laugh. She makes everyone in a room smile."

"Yeah, what's not to like about Molly?" Darby defended her brand-new acquaintance. "Not liking Molly is a little like saying you dislike cotton candy at the amusement park or sno-cones at the mall."

"Maybe," Izzy said grudgingly, "but I still think she's strange. She looks as though she fixes her hair by sticking her finger into an electrical outlet."

Darby couldn't argue with that. Molly's hair was curly to the point of unmanageable frizz and haloed around her head like a yellow glow. Still, Darby had a hunch that Molly had considerably more substance than the human equivalent to cotton candy or sno-cones. There was definitely more to Molly Ashton than first met the eye.

At that moment, Darby caught Jake's eye, and a grin melted across his face. Darby felt her insides dissolving along with it. There were many reasons she was glad to be a part of this program—and one of them was looking at her right now.

"We almost forgot to tell you about Sarah Riley—" Izzy was cut short by a sharp cry. Mrs. Oakland began panting as fast as she could, and Izzy's eyes grew round as saucers.

"The baby . . . it's coming!"

CHAPTER 3

LIVE
FROM BRENTWOOD HIGH

"Oh boy, oh boy, oh boy!" Izzy's breath began coming in spurts almost as short as Mrs. Oakland's. "Now what?"

The scream of an ambulance siren cut through his question.

"That's the sweetest sound I've ever heard. Quick, Jake! Get the door!"

The room erupted into action as two emergency medical technicians raced inside. With a practiced eye, they assessed the situation.

"How far apart are the pains?" The young EMT didn't appear any older than Jake or Izzy, but his intent expression gave him a maturity beyond his years.

"The last couple have been a minute and a half apart," Jake responded.

"I'm having another contraction!" Mrs. Oakland announced into the confusion.

"That was one minute from the last one," Jake said shakily. He stared at his watch. "Is that possible?"

"It certainly is. This baby is on its way. There's no time to move her," the older man assessed. "Let's get ready for a delivery."

"Oh boy, oh boy, oh boy . . ."

"Izzy, will you *shut up*?" Darby said in exasperation.

"Pull yourself together, Izz," Jake ordered. "Are you taking notes? Make yourself useful. We need to get this down for our story."

As Darby, Jake, and Izzy moved out of the way to make room for the brisk, professional movements of the EMTs, Darby focused her attention on the young man talking gently to Mrs. Oakland. He was tenderly brushing the damp hair away from her forehead with his hand.

"Everything is going to be fine, ma'am. We'll transport you as soon as the baby is born. If you can relax, things will be easier for you. Breathe deeply. Just remember, having a baby isn't like being ill. This is the most natural thing in the world. A God-given miracle." His voice was calm, conversational, as if he had discussions just like this one every single day.

"Grady," Mrs. Oakland panted, "these are the kids from Brentwood High. I wanted you to meet them. . . . Here comes another pain. . . ."

"Breathe out, two, three." The young man was completely focused on his patient. "Breathe in, two, three. That's it. You're doing a good job. No problem here. Where's your bedroom? We should make you more comfortable."

"I don't think there's time," Mrs. Oakland gasped. "Besides, we have a waterbed. I don't think I could push . . ."

"The floor then." In a moment, the men had spread quilts and afghans across the carpet and had Mrs. Oakland lowered to the floor and out of sight.

"We'd better go—" Jake offered.

"No, no!" Mrs. Oakland's disembodied voice drifted upward from the floor. "Your story . . ."

Darby and the boys backed themselves as far away from the center of activity as they could. From their position, only the young EMT's back was visible.

"He's good," Izzy whispered. "Are you *sure* he's our age?"

Darby swallowed the thick lump in her throat and brushed the back of her hand against her forehead. She was surprised to feel cold, sticky perspiration there.

She glanced at Jake's ashen face. He ran unsteady fingers through his already disheveled hair. He was beginning to look as pale and rumpled as an unmade bed.

Mrs. Oakland's breathing grew faster and heavier. The EMTs moved calmly and with precision. Their professional presence was comforting.

"I'm monitoring the baby's heartbeat with my stethoscope. It's nice and strong, Mrs. Oakland. About 140 beats a minute. Perfect."

"Grady, pull out an obstetric pack," the older EMT ordered. "Pant, ma'am. That's right. Keep it up. A couple more contractions and we're going to have a new visitor."

"The baby, it's coming!"

"Sure is, Mrs. Oakland. Keep breathing. Pant with the contractions. You're doing great. The head's just about ready to deliver. Time to push."

A soft groan drew Darby's attention. Izzy, his brawny body slack, was propped against a nearby wall. He moaned again.

"I think I'm going to throw up," Izzy whispered through gritted teeth. His complexion was industrial gray, the color of cement blocks and washed rock. "We should never have come."

"Okay, Mrs. Oakland, time to push. This baby wants to be born."

Darby reached for Izzy's hand, and immediately her slender fingers were engulfed by his huge calloused paw. At the same moment, Jake grabbed her other hand.

"Good job. Everything is going according to plan. Keep up the good work. Okay, time to push." The older EMT kept up a constant, comforting patter as he worked with Mrs. Oakland, his kindly voice soothing the unwilling visitors huddled in the far corner as well as his patient. "I'm just supporting the baby's head. Here comes the body. Any guesses whether it will be a girl or a boy?"

Though they could see nothing of Mrs. Oakland, Grady was visible, readying the equipment for the baby's delivery. He laid out a receiving blanket, tape, scissors, a rubber suction syringe, and several items that Darby did not recognize. Grady was calm and collected, as though delivering babies was what he did every day. There was no hint that he was actually a high-school senior who, if not for being on ambulance call, might be shooting hoops with his friends or bagging groceries at the local supermarket.

"Do you think we'll get extra credit for this?" Izzy asked, his voice faint, "or kicked out of the program entirely?"

"Push!"

Mrs. Oakland made an enthusiastic noise halfway between a laugh and a cry. Suddenly a foreign noise filled the room.

"Waaaaahhhh!"

"It's a *boy*!"

At the sound, Izzy's shaggy head thumped loudly against the wall. He slid down the wall, back to plaster, until he hit the floor. His knees were spread wide, one on each side of his ears, as he clenched his hands tightly together in front of him. "A baby," he whispered. "A real baby."

"Of course it is!" Jake prodded Izzy with the toe of his boot. "Stand up."

"I can't. I might faint. Ms. Wright is going to wring our necks. . . ."

Izzy reached for a ceramic crock filled with magazines near his shoulder. He dumped the magazines on the floor and promptly threw up in the crock.

"Izzy!"

"Don't talk to me . . . I'm dying." He moaned and leaned his head against the wall.

Darby tuned out Izzy's complaints as she watched Grady take the baby aside to study him thoroughly. The tiny lump of blankets squirmed and bleated. As though he could feel her eyes on him, Grady glanced up.

"I'm evaluating the baby," he explained as he worked, "with the Apgar scoring system. It's a system of zero to ten with ten being the highest score."

"What do you look for?" Darby was surprised at how shaky her voice sounded in her own ears.

"Color. The baby should be nice and pink like this one. A baby who is pale or bluish in color is probably in distress."

Darby stared at the squalling infant, which Grady had swaddled in something he'd called a "bubble bag." The child was covered with a white, cheesy substance from the birth, but she could actually see the baby's tender skin pinking up as he cried.

"We also check heart rate, muscle tone, reflexes, and respiratory effort. This little guy is definitely a ten."

Grady wrote some comments down on a chart, then began checking the baby again.

"Newborns lose their body heat rapidly." Grady took a second blanket from the obstetric pack and wrapped the baby in it. "We want to protect him from heat loss to maintain his energy. It's easier to keep a baby warm than it is to warm a cold infant."

Then Grady gently laid the child in his mother's arms. Darby moved forward to see Mrs. Oakland turn back a corner of the blanket and look adoringly into the child's eyes. Suddenly the baby's squalling stopped. Dark blue eyes, only minutes old, connected with his mother's pale green ones. Mother and son had met.

"Are you crying?" Izzy whispered as he struggled to stand and join Darby. "Is everything okay?"

"Everything is perfect. Absolutely perfect. We just witnessed a miracle, Izz. A real, true-to-life miracle."

"*You* might have. I didn't see a thing." Izzy hugged his stocky middle. "My stomach hurts."

As Mrs. Oakland and son were being transported to the waiting ambulance its flashing red light bathed the room in a rose-tinge glow. Darby's notebook lay forgotten on the countertop nearby. Already she was mentally working on the story evolving around this dramatic scene.

"Wow! What a story *that* will make!" Sarah Riley's

wheelchair bumped Darby's leg as she maneuvered into position beside her friend. "I can't believe your good luck—a firsthand account of a teen EMT in action! I wish I'd been there."

"Me too. Izzy was no help at all. I thought he was going to faint and *he'd* be the one in the ambulance."

"Sometimes I get so mad at this metal monster!" Sarah frowned as she made a sweeping gesture that encompassed her wheelchair. A helium-filled balloon floated from one of the handgrips. Her schoolbag hung empty on the back of the chair because Sarah had wedged all her books alongside of her. "If my customized van hadn't been in the shop, I could have driven out to Braddington too!"

Darby looked at Sarah in surprise, taken aback by the outburst.

Sarah rarely complained about her handicap, instinctively aware of the barrier the chair created and of the distance it put between her and others her age. She always tried to minimize its effect as much as possible and kept it approachable and unintimidating by decorating it with balloons, ribbons, cutout comics, posters, or whatever struck her fancy. Still, there was no doubt that the chair remained a barrier.

Though Darby and Sarah had shared several classes, there was much about Sarah that Darby didn't know. Darby felt a sudden pang of guilt for allowing that to be the case. Sarah had always been outgoing and friendly toward her. Now that they were working on *Live! From Brentwood High* together, she would make an extra effort to get to know Sarah.

"There will be other chances to get good stories," Darby assured the auburn-haired girl. "I'm sure of it."

"I hope so. I applied for the Brentwood High program because I really want to learn about journalism and the print medium. I want to be a writer—but the chance to witness a birth! Wow!"

"We didn't actually witness anything. We stayed out of the way. Still, it was awesome watching the EMTs work. It's hard to believe that Grady O'Brien is only a little older than we are."

"What did Ms. Wright say about your experience?"

"Nothing, yet. I'm sure she's heard about it through the grapevine. You know how Izzy babbles. I'm on my way to talk to her now. Do you think she'll be mad?"

"Nah. She's cool. I like her. If you don't give Ms. Wright any trouble, she won't give you any either."

Darby touched the bright balloon hovering just over Sarah's head. "What's the fascination with this? Did the ribbons you had laced through your wheel spokes fall off?"

An impish light gleamed in Sarah's eyes. "It gets me to class more quickly. Everyone gets out of the way for the 'balloon lady.' Besides, yellow is my favorite color."

Sarah glanced at her wristwatch. "Gotta go. I need to get started before the bell rings or I'll end up stuck in traffic. See you later?"

"Sure." Darby paused. "Maybe we could get together sometime?"

"I'd like that." Sarah's pleasure at the suggestion spread across her features. "I'd like it a lot." With surprising strength for one so petite, Sarah grasped the wheel rim on her chair and propelled herself forward. She turned her head to call over her shoulder, "Don't forget!"

Darby smiled as she watched the girl maneuver

down the hall. There was something special about Sarah. She couldn't quite put her finger on it, but there was almost a . . . glow . . . about her. Sarah was always happy, cheerful, and upbeat even though she had more reasons than most to be gloomy or sad. Suddenly Darby was anxious to learn to know Sarah better and to find out what her secret might be.

––––––––––

"Door's open. Don't knock unless you plan to do something about it."

Darby's eyes widened at the blunt invitation into Ms. Wright's office. Ms. Wright was definitely one-of-a-kind, unlike any of the other teachers at Brentwood High. She often wore batik-print clothing made in India and thick-soled sandals, her long brown hair pulled into a ponytail. She usually sported pierced earrings that looked as though they'd been made at the elementary school down the street. Occasionally, however, she had been spotted in the halls in dark-colored power suits, heels, and proper little gold earrings. Rumor had it that Ms. Wright liked to keep everyone just a little off-kilter and unsure of themselves around her.

She'd been a television producer for a small midwestern station before coming to Brentwood. There she'd developed a knack for what some of her students called "X-ray vision." Darby wasn't quite sure how to approach a teacher who could see right through her to the nerves jangling in her stomach.

"Well, what are you waiting for? Christmas?" Ms. Wright, who appeared to be somewhere between thirty-five and forty, thrust herself away from a desk piled high with papers, tapes, and clutter, stopped the rolling chair with the toe of her sandal and spun eighty degrees so that she faced directly at Darby.

"I don't imagine you came here to discuss my charming personality or my fashion sense," Ms. Wright observed, "so what can I do for you?"

Darby couldn't seem to take her eyes off the bulletin board behind Ms. Wright. It was covered with newsclippings, memorabilia, and black-and-white photos, all of Ms. Wright with famous people—including a former President.

"Do you like my scrapbook?" Ms. Wright looked amused. "One without pages, of course. Pages are too much bother to turn. This way I can look at my life without leaving my desk."

Then, changing subjects quickly, Ms. Wright added, "I hear you had an exciting afternoon this past weekend."

"So Izzy already told you."

"Not Izzy . . . Mrs. Oakland. She called me from the hospital. Said my research team had gotten more than they'd bargained for."

"We tried to stay out of the way . . ."

"Oh, she didn't mind. She's so proud of the EMT program and her students taking part that she'd probably have let you film the whole thing. Too bad you didn't have Gary with you on Saturday."

Darby's blank look spurred Ms. Wright to elaborate. "Gary Richmond will be working with me on the program. He's a cameraman and will help to tape the features. I hope he'll be at tomorrow's meeting. Are you ready to start writing your story?"

"Oh, no!" Darby gasped. "Not at all. Because of the baby's birth, we didn't get a chance to interview the

EMTs. I never realized how much there was to learn."

"I'm glad you've already begun to realize the importance of accurate, in-depth research. The on-camera stuff is the easy part in this business. Most of what happens in television goes on *behind* the scenes. Research. Writing. Very unglamorous. And we can't forget the technical workers who put the show on the air—camera people, directors, producers, the person who runs the TelePrompTer and the switcher, the lighting people . . ." Suddenly Ms. Wright grinned. "Sorry. I got carried away. See you at our meeting tomorrow?"

Darby nodded and backed toward the door, her head spinning. "Tomorrow."

———

The meeting room provided for the *Live! From Brentwood High* staff looked as though an explosion had recently occurred within its walls. Posters hung at odd angles, a curtain sagged from its rod, dead and dying plants lined the windowsills. Students milled about the room. Someone had scrawled the words "Media Zoo" on the walls.

Almost hidden by the crowd was a trompe l'oeil rendition of windows looking out onto a sunny meadow. Darby could see a cow peeking in through one imaginary window, a horse in another.

Someone in the art department had a sense of humor. Brentwood High School sat in the busiest part of the city, far removed from anything that looked even faintly like a pasture. Of course, this particular room didn't exactly resemble a classroom either.

"May I have your attention—or else!"

Silence spread across the room like a ripple, starting at Ms. Wright's desk and finally reaching back to the far corners of the room.

"As you may have heard, three members of Team One had an exciting experience this weekend."

"Hey, Izzy! I heard you passed out cold!" someone joked from the back of the room.

"You heard wrong," Izzy growled, but he blushed red to the roots of his stubbly hair.

"He didn't pass out. He barfed! Izzy's got a *delicate* stomach!"

Izzy might have defended himself, but at that moment, the door flew open, and a rough, disheveled-looking man in scuffed sandals and tattered jeans burst into the room; his long brown hair sailed out behind his shoulders as he walked. Instinctively Darby gathered her books to her chest. *Who in the world is this?*

CHAPTER 4

LIVE

FROM DRENTWOOD HIGH

The man halted in front of Ms. Wright's desk. "Sorry I'm late." He winked. "I overslept."

It looked possible—even though it was after three in the afternoon. The man's jawline was shadowed by stubble; he wore a Celtics cap worn backward and a wrinkled Yankees sweatshirt. He was disreputable looking, yet strangely appealing.

"I'd like you to meet Gary Richmond," Ms. Wright began. "Gary is a professional cameraman. He'll be taping the stories you research and write."

Richmond would be a very handsome man if he weren't so weary looking, Darby decided. Though he seemed relaxed and at ease bantering with Ms. Wright, there was a tiredness about him that seemed more than physical. Though Gary appeared to be about thirty years old, his eyes looked a hundred.

"Gary will be our field producer. We're fortunate to have someone with his credentials willing to work on this program. He's worked with national television news teams for several years as well as having spent time as a photojournalist. Gary has spent most of the last few years abroad, covering world events such as the Gulf crisis, the airlifts into Somalia, and the civil war in Bosnia."

"So what's he doing here?" Andrew Tremaine asked with a silky snideness. "Why would anyone who's supposedly done all that stoop to playing television with a bunch of high-school kids?"

"They pay me enough and I'll do anything," Gary answered levelly, his eyes never leaving Andrew's face as he pulled up a chair and sat down.

A blush crept from the base of Andrew's neck, across his cheeks, and into his hairline.

"Score one point for Richmond," Izzy commented near Darby's ear. "I like him already."

"Gary knows you've been given your first assignments," Ms. Wright said. "He is aware that you'll be working in print as well as broadcast mediums. Fortunately, he's also had experience as a still photographer and is willing to work with you in all areas. Use Gary as a resource. He can teach you a great deal. You'll be developing your own story ideas, so I recommend that you keep your eyes and ears open."

"What if we can't find anything interesting to report?"

"News is everywhere. You'll have to find it, just as three of your classmates did this weekend in Braddington."

Someone in the back row tittered. Another began humming a lullaby. Izzy blushed.

"That's what this program is all about—seeing the world with a journalist's eye. Finding the story. Reporting the facts. Making people care." An amused smile played on Ms. Wright's lips as she viewed the nervous expressions on her students' faces. "I didn't say it would be easy."

She turned to Richmond, who sat slumped in his chair, looking half asleep. "Gary, the students have been divided into research teams. Team assignments are not permanent. Since we have so many stories to cover, a student may participate on more than one team at a time. It may seem confusing at first, but I'm sure that once you get to know everyone, it will be easier."

Ms. Wright looked out at the classroom. "Since Team One is the only group who've already begun their research, I'd like the rest of you to get into your groups and start discussing your game plans. Gary and I will answer any questions you might have. Team One, you can take this time to plan your next step."

Slowly the groups in the room broke apart and re-arranged themselves according to their assigned teams. Molly Ashton joined Darby, Izzy, and Jake on the far side of the room.

"Why'd we have to get Andrew Tremaine in our group?" she whispered.

"Yeah, why'd *we* have to get stuck with the biggest ego in three states?" Izzy added.

Andrew was conceited and egotistical—and not ex-actly a team player. When he'd been invited to drive to Braddington last Saturday, he'd announced that he had better things to do than ride around in an ambulance with a bunch of country hicks.

Andrew might be a wasted effort, Darby mused, but it was awfully nice to be on the same team as Jake. He was definitely worth getting to know better.

Sarah gently bumped against Darby's leg with the

wheel of her chair. "I'm glad we're together," she whispered. "This is all a little scary."

"I know what you mean."

Ms. Wright and Mr. Richmond weren't like any of the instructors Darby had had before. Their lives hadn't been spent in classrooms. They'd lived everything they'd come to teach. After the emotion-packed experience she'd had on Saturday, Darby wasn't completely sure if she were up to learning what they had to offer.

" . . . and by the way," Ms. Wright said, "when you come here, you are no longer in school. You are at *work*. You are expected to behave like professionals. This is *not* the place to search for prom dates. We have stories to research and to write. If you do a second-rate job you will be publicly embarrassed. After all, your names will be in the credits. That should inspire you to do your best. It's what I expect. *Your best*. We have one of the finest cameramen in the country working with us. You've been chosen for this program from dozens of applicants. Now show me what you can do."

Ms. Wright descended upon Team One with her class book open. "Since your group has a head start, your news feature will be scheduled first. Can you have it put together in two weeks?"

"Two weeks? We'll need two months!" Molly groaned after Ms. Wright moved to another group. "Nobody told me this was going to be so hard!"

"Or you would have stayed away," Andrew sneered. "Wimp."

Molly's eyes narrowed and she shot him a daggered look. "It takes one to know one, Andrew."

Fortunately, Ms. Wright began to speak before Andrew had time to formulate a retort.

"The format for a ninety-second story has, as does any story, a beginning, middle, and end. Introduce your story, give the majority of your material in the body, and wrap it up with a tight, memorable conclusion. If you have any questions about format, you can bring them to class next Monday afternoon."

"Class?" Andrew blurted. "Do we have to be there?"

Ms. Wright lifted an eyebrow. "You mean you already know everything you need to know about television production? Excuse me. I thought it might be helpful to introduce a little about camera angles, picture composition, audio, lighting techniques, switching ... but maybe I'm boring you. For those of you who aren't already experts like Mr. Tremaine here, we'll use class time to introduce you to all the areas of production. Over the course of the program, each of you will have the opportunity to experience every job required to produce the story.

"Stay alert. The news is now your job. It's everywhere. All you have to do is find it, to see that unique angle, that human interest story which makes it important to the public and to put it out there for all to see."

Ms. Wright shuffled through the papers in her arms. "Here's a sample broadcast script. Take a look at it. The next one you see will be written by you. They must be turned in for advance approval before you begin taping. If I'm not available, talk to Gary."

Darby looked uncertainly at Izzy, whose befuddled expression mirrored her own.

"Can we do this?" Molly put into words the thought in everyone's minds.

"Of course you can." Gary had come up behind them. "Don't be intimidated by something new. You may surprise yourselves and become hooked on the industry. That's what happened to me."

"What were you doing before you got 'hooked'?" Molly tipped her frizzy blond head to one side.

"Majoring in English literature. A photography class I'd taken for the fun of it made me realize that there is more than one way of communicating with the public."

After Gary moved away, Andrew allowed his cynical expression to grow more apparent. "Big help he's going to be. Looks like a guy who got trapped in the seventies."

"Don't be so negative, Andy," Izzy said.

"My name is *Andrew*."

"Right." Izzy paused. "Andy."

While the two boys faced each other in a glare-down, Molly threw her hands into the air. "I should have signed up for the Advanced Foods class! At least there I wouldn't have had to listen to you two fighting."

Sarah wheeled her chair between the two antagonists and pleaded, "Break it up, you guys."

"Mind your own business," Andrew snapped.

"Get a life, Andy," came Izzy's quick response.

"Hey, I don't have to take this . . ."

This was a news *team*? Darby wondered as the discussion deteriorated. Things were looking very grim.

CHAPTER 5

LIVE

FROM BRENTWOOD HIGH

"I'm getting out of here!" Andrew flung his notebook onto the desk as the dismissal bell rang half an hour later. He left the room with Molly hard on his heels, muttering something about the biggest mistake of her life.

The room emptied quickly. Darby, Izzy, and Jake remained behind.

"Well," Jake commented. "What do you think?"

"About ... the ... the internship program?" Darby stammered.

"What else?"

Much as she hated to admit it, Darby had already forgotten about the program. Instead, she'd been thinking about Jake's smile.

"You're acting weird, Darby," Izzy said bluntly. "What's the deal?"

She wasn't quite sure. Boys had never been much of a problem to her. Darby'd had plenty of them as friends and had as many dates as she was interested in having, but none had affected her quite like this.

Darby prided herself on her clear, logical mind. Jake Saunders' presence had muddled that with one green-eyed wink.

She passed her hand over her eyes. "Sorry. My mind is boggled. I'm in over my head."

"You and me both." Izzy slumped against the wall. "I might as well give up now."

"Don't be an idiot. We'll be fine—all of us. There are six people in our group. If we work together, we'll make it."

"Jake's right. All we have to do is put our heads together."

"Yeah, Izzy," Jake agreed. "We could do it with your head alone if you'd quit worrying."

"Very funny," Izzy growled as he stomped toward the door. "Let's find the others."

"I wish Izzy would give himself a little credit." Jake gathered his books and turned to Darby. "For an off-the-charts genius, he's certainly insecure."

Darby nodded and smiled. Izzy was a big, bumbling teddy bear who turned into a royal klutz when there was a pretty girl in the room. It was difficult to remember he was a genius when most of the time he acted like such a dope.

"Are you guys coming?" Izzy poked his head back into the classroom. "I've got Andrew, Molly, and Sarah out here in the hall. We need to talk."

Andrew looked up sullenly as Jake and Darby entered the hallway. He was obviously there under duress. Molly didn't look much happier than Andrew. Her large blue eyes were brimming with concern. Only Sarah seemed tranquil.

"Okay, guys," Izzy addressed the group. "We've got no time for goofing off. When do you want to meet and plan our strategy?"

"How about right now?" Sarah suggested. "At the

coffee shop in the mall. That's only a few blocks away."

"Now?" Andrew whined. "What's the rush?"

"We're eager to spend time in your company, Tre-maine," Izzy retorted. "You and Jake can ride with me. We'll see you at Cafe Espresso in twenty minutes." He dragged the two boys away, leaving Darby, Molly, and Sarah staring after them.

"Do you mind riding with me?" Sarah asked. "I've got my van."

The girls followed Sarah to the parking lot. In the handicapped parking sat a full-sized burgundy van with black trim. "This is it." Sarah looked at the vehicle fondly. "My world-expanding dream mobile."

"What does that mean?" Molly scrutinized the or-dinary-looking vehicle.

"Watch." Sarah wheeled to the side of the van and opened the large sliding door by hitting a switch on the outside of the van. Inside was a platform that slowly unfolded outward until it projected away from the ve-hicle.

Sarah positioned herself on the slotted floor of the lift, and with the push of a button on the post at her side, Sarah and wheelchair rose to the height of the van's floor. With experienced maneuvering, Sarah backed her wheelchair into the van and swung around to face the steering wheel. A lock system secured the wheelchair in place.

She dipped into the pocket of her sweater and pulled out a set of keys. "Well, are you coming?"

Molly and Darby scrambled into the vehicle. Darby sat in the back while Molly took the passenger seat next to Sarah. Sarah touched another button, which brought the lift back into the van and shut the door.

"Neat! So you can drive this all by yourself?"

"It was customized just for me. Here's the hand-operated gas pedal, and the brake. . . ." Sarah proudly pointed out all the features of the van. "That's why I call it my 'dream machine.' After my accident, I was afraid that I'd never be able to do anything 'normal' ever again. Sometimes the fact that I can actually drive blows me away."

"I always wondered how you got to school," Molly admitted. "Who taught you to drive? It's not exactly like you could sign up for Drivers' Ed., is it?"

"I spent several weeks at a rehabilitation hospital in Denver after the accident," Sarah explained as she pulled out of the parking lot. "They taught me lots of things there, including how to drive. The day I got home from the hospital, my dad had the dream machine sitting in the driveway, waiting for me. I couldn't believe my eyes. I knew how much my family had spent on my hospital care and that they couldn't afford something as expensive as this van. I was terrified that I'd be dependent on others to get around for the rest of my life.

"When I learned that the van was a gift from my dad's company and that all the employees had donated money to have it customized for me, I knew for sure that it was a miracle."

Darby began to realize just how much the freedom to drive meant to Sarah. "Aren't your parents worried about your driving?"

"My parents are determined to make me totally independent. Crazy, isn't it? If I weren't in a wheelchair they'd probably never let me have my own car!"

Molly's gaze drifted over the metal skeleton of the

wheelchair and Sarah's motionless legs. "I thought that someone like you wouldn't believe in miracles—not after what happened to you."

Sarah smiled serenely. "Oh, miracles happen all the time. You just have to look for them in order to see them."

Molly looked at Sarah doubtfully, not quite understanding Sarah's strange response. "I remember when your accident happened," she blurted.

In the backseat, Darby groaned and sank back against the seat. *Keep your mouth shut, Molly. Don't remind her.*

They had stopped at a red light, and a fleeting expression of pain flitted across Sarah's features. Then she composed herself and her serene expression returned. "It was a terrible time."

Molly, who was famous for putting her mouth in gear before her brain, pressed on. "I read about it in the paper. The headline read, 'BRENTWOOD GIRL INJURED IN BICYCLE ACCIDENT.' That was you, wasn't it?"

"That was me, all right. I was on my way home from the grocery store with a pound of butter. My mom was baking cookies and she'd run out." Sarah's voice softened with the memory. "I told her I'd hurry back. We were going to take the cookies to a picnic at the church. The cookies never got there. Neither did I."

"You don't need to tell us. . . ." Darby interrupted.

Sarah shook her head as she drove through the intersection. "It's okay. I can talk about it now. For a long time I didn't want to remember, but now I've accepted who I am. I'm Sarah Riley and I'm a paraplegic. That's the first thing people notice about me—the wheelchair.

I've had to get used to it. To most people, I'm handicapped first and a person second."

"I didn't mean it that way!" Molly protested.

"I know. But I understand your curiosity. I'd be curious too if our positions were reversed." Sarah flipped on the turn signal and maneuvered around the corner. "Sometimes, when I feel left out of things, I try to put myself in others' shoes to help me understand how they must feel about me and my handicap."

"Do you feel left out a lot?" Molly's voice was little more than a whisper.

An interminable pause told them more than they wanted to know.

"I feel *terrible!*" Molly blurted. "I guess I never even thought about *your* feelings!"

"I'd probably be wary of someone in a wheelchair too. Don't blame yourself. I understand why some kids never try to get to know me—and some who used to be my friends seem uncomfortable now." There was a wistfulness in Sarah's tone that betrayed her emotion. "It does get a little lonely though, sometimes."

"What a bunch of jerks we are! You had a terrible accident, and we've made it so much worse."

"Actually, the accident wasn't such a big deal. The car that hit me was only going twenty miles an hour. It just grazed my bike. I think everyone was surprised I couldn't just get up and walk away. I know I was."

"I'm sorry I'm so thoughtless," Molly moaned. "And I promise to do better in the future. Unless, of course, you think I'd make things worse. Then please tell me to mind my own business."

The cheerful sound of Sarah's laughter filled the van. "Molly, I *am* your business now—and you are mine. We're a news team. We'd better learn to understand each other, right?"

Molly gave Sarah an admiring glance. "You know what? You're something else."

"Am I supposed to say 'thank you' for that?"

"Sure. It was a compliment." Molly grinned. "You really handle this wheelchair thing well."

"Not always," Sarah admitted, "but I'm learning."

Sarah was amazing—graciously attempting to make people comfortable with her wheelchair. Darby wasn't sure she'd be able to do that if she were in Sarah's position. Another point for Sarah. Darby grew more intrigued by her new acquaintance all the time.

"What a loser I am." Molly thrust a hand into her purse and drew out a powder compact and flipped it open. She stared into the tiny mirror, chanting, "Loser. Loser. Loser."

"What's that supposed to mean?"

"I can't do anything right. First Blake, now Sarah."

"Whoa! Stop right there!" Sarah said sternly. "What did I do to deserve being put into the same category as Blake Denton?"

"See what I mean? I insulted you again!"

"Would somebody like to explain this conversation to me?" Darby asked. "What's this about you and Blake? Izzy said something about you two breaking up, but . . ."

Blake Denton and Molly had been going together for nearly eight months. Everyone around Brentwood High knew them as a couple.

"He dumped me." Molly stared into the compact mirror. "He decided I wasn't his 'type.' He decided that April Hennessy *was* his type instead. How do you think

I'd look with long black hair and big brown eyes?"

"When did this happen?"

"A couple weeks ago."

"Sorry."

"You and me both. I thought he loved me. Boy, was I wrong!" Molly made a face at the mirror. "How do you think I'd look if I dyed my hair? Maybe just a little darker . . . with some highlights. Maybe some new makeup too. I . . ."

"You look just fine the way you are," Sarah insisted. "Perfect. Beautiful. Why would you want to change a thing?"

"Blake said—"

"Who listens to him? He's got no taste. He dumped *you*, didn't he?"

"But maybe he's right. If I lost five pounds and got some new clothes, it might help."

"Molly! Are you crazy? You look wonderful the way you are. Blake was just grabbing at straws, trying to find things to criticize about you so it would be easier for him to break it off. You can't pay any attention to that."

"But I did," Molly said in a small voice. "I keep hearing what he said over and over in my mind. And every time I replay it, I feel worse."

Sarah glanced helplessly at Darby in the rearview mirror.

"I'm really excited about the internship, aren't you?" Darby ventured, hoping to change the subject. "Just think, maybe one of us will actually *be* in the television business some day!"

"Not me," Molly stated. "At least not in the *news* portion."

"Then what are you doing in the program?"

"I want to be a model or a movie star," Molly announced grandly. "And you don't have to tell me I'm nuts. My parents and family have already told me. Blake too—about a dozen times the night we broke up. Still, I think I can do it if I plan things right. I'm going to college to get a degree in business first. That way I'll be able to manage my own career. I wanted to be a part of this program because it will look good on my resume."

"I didn't realize you'd thought so much about your future," Darby murmured. "I'm impressed."

"Besides, now that I'm free, I just happened to notice that there are some *great*-looking guys in the program—Jake Saunders, Shane Donahue . . . even Andy Tremaine. Of course, Andy doesn't need *me* in his fan club. His ego is already big enough to fill it."

Darby felt Sarah's amused gaze upon her in the rearview mirror. Darby shrugged and Sarah grinned.

Deftly changing the subject, Sarah asked, "Did I hear you say *Andy* Tremaine?"

"I know. Did you see his face when Izzy called him 'Andy' in class? He hates it when anyone does that. Makes him feel too ordinary, I guess. Good for Izzy, though. Andy *needs* to feel ordinary."

"Maybe," Sarah countered, "but I think it's rather nice to realize that each of us is *extraordinary* too— different, unique. We really should be celebrating that instead of running down people who stand out in some way or another."

It was the kind of statement Darby had come to expect from Sarah. She always looked at the world through optimistic eyes. Just being around Sarah always made Darby feel a little better!

With a start, Darby realized that they were already at the mall. She felt herself studying Sarah curiously as the three of them made their way to the cafe. What was it about Sarah that made her so unique? Her handicap? Her attitude? Or something deeper?

"You're late," Izzy accused when the girls arrived at Cafe Espresso. "We've been here ten minutes. . . ."

"And two ice cream sundaes ago," Andrew added. "This boy eats like a hog."

"I'm still growing. I have to keep my energy level high."

"If you keep eating like that, you're going to have to change your career plans," Jake commented as he slid his chair to the side to make room for Darby. "Instead of becoming a producer of documentaries, you'll have to become a sumo wrestler. Then at least you'll have an excuse for weighing five hundred pounds."

"I'll ignore that statement," Izzy said with dignity. "And I think I'll have a banana split."

When everyone had ordered, Darby reached for the notebook and pen she had carried into the cafe. "Okay, I'm ready," she announced, pen poised over paper. "What's our plan?"

"We should decide what is left to do and then divide up the work," Sarah suggested. She rapped her knuckles on the wheelchair. "Since I'm attached to this thing, why don't I do research? I can make some calls and find out the history of the emergency medical technician program and what's involved in becoming an EMT. Maybe Molly and Andy—Andrew—could help me."

"Sounds good to me," Molly said.

Andrew gave a guttural grunt that everyone assumed meant yes.

"Okay, Jake, Darby, and I will do the legwork. Since we met the EMTs at Mrs. Oakland's, we can line up an interview."

"And once we've pulled it all together, we can have Gary come with us to tape the story."

"This should be fun!"

"You'd probably think having a tooth pulled is fun too!"

"Oh, Andrew, don't be like that!" Molly pleaded. "We really want you to work with us. Besides, I need an A to bring up my grade point average. If you refuse to work, it will affect all of us!"

"Don't try to butter him up," Izzy cautioned. "He's not going to listen anyway."

"Let her try. She might convince me." He leered at the girl. "Right, Molly?"

How could anyone so good-looking be such a jerk? Darby wondered. Andrew Tremaine was proof positive that looks weren't everything. Cocky. Self-assured. Selfish. Smart but too lazy to apply the brains he'd been given. And a terrible flirt.

"Maybe the two of us could go to the library," Andrew continued, "and . . ." He slid his arm across Molly's shoulders in a suggestive manner.

" . . . and you'll let her do all the work," Izzy finished for him. "No way, buddy. Everybody carries their own weight in this group. And keep your hands off the staff." His eyes rested on Andrew's arm.

Molly looked stiff and miserable.

"That puts the most responsibility on you then," Andrew retorted, slowly withdrawing the offending arm, "considering your size and appetite."

Izzy's eyes narrowed and his hands curled into fists, ready to rearrange Andrew's face for him. Quickly, Darby put her hands, palms down, on top of Izzy's tightened knuckles.

"Stop it, you two. Fighting isn't going to get us anywhere. We've got two weeks to pull together the best story Channel 9 has ever seen. Right?"

No one answered her. Izzy and Andrew continued to glare at each other while Molly and Sarah stared worriedly at one boy and then the other. Jake, obviously disgusted, pushed his chair away from the table.

How were they ever going to become a team?

CHAPTER 6

LIVE

FROM BRENTWOOD HIGH

"Are you ready?" Izzy peered at Darby through the crack in the front door.

"Come in. I've got to get my jacket." Darby grabbed for the denim and twill coat draped over a chair. "Am I dressed up enough to go to the hospital?"

"You look okay to me."

"Thanks. A compliment from a guy who looks like he chose his clothes after an explosion in a clothing store."

"If you don't trust me don't ask." Izzy shrugged carelessly, not in the least insulted by Darby's teasing. "Hurry up. Jake's waiting in the car."

"This is a little weird," Izzy commented as they pulled into the visitor parking lot at the hospital. "The last time we saw Mrs. Oakland she was having a baby."

"It's going to be fun," Darby assured him. "Come on."

They made their way through a maze of doors and hallways to the nursery. Several people were already standing at the bank of windows, staring in at the infants lined up in cribs. Mrs. Oakland was one of them.

"Hello, there!" she greeted them. "Did you come to visit Franklin James Oakland the third?"

"And you, too. Oh! Is that him?" A beautiful pink baby swaddled in a blue blanket stared back at Darby from his crib.

"Isn't he something? I'm glad you came. We're going home tomorrow. In fact, we should be home already, but little Frank's bilirubin count was high, so we had to stay a little longer."

"Is he going to be all right?"

"Just fine. No problem. So, how's the story coming?"

"So far your interview has been the most exciting."

"I would imagine so." Mrs. Oakland chuckled. "It was exciting for me too."

"We brought you something." Izzy thrust a package into Mrs. Oakland's hand. It was crudely wrapped, and Darby wished fleetingly that she'd offered to buy and wrap the gift. Who knew what Izzy might think appropriate for a tiny infant?

"How nice of you! I'll open it right now." Mrs. Oakland tore into the package and lifted out a tiny blue T-shirt with the words *Live! From Brentwood High* emblazoned across the front.

"Sorry the letters are so small," Izzy apologized, "but babies don't have very big chests."

"It's absolutely perfect. I love it!" Mrs. Oakland beamed at all of them. "Thank you for the gift." She peered back through the nursery window. "The nurse is picking up the baby. Want a closer look?"

They moved toward the window to peer at the infant. His little pink mouth worked and puckered like that of a baby sparrow.

"Look at the size of his hands!" Jake commented in awe. "And the fingernails!"

"Imagine anything that small and complicated being so perfect." Izzy stared at the baby as if he were seeing one for the first time.

"It's a miracle," Mrs. Oakland said reverently. "No one will ever be able to convince me otherwise. God has a hand in this."

Izzy leaned his forehead on the cool glass window, entranced by the baby. "Are you scared?"

Darby and Jake glanced at each other, surprised by Izzy's odd question. Only Mrs. Oakland seemed to understand.

"A little. I feel like a thousand pounds of responsibility has landed on my shoulders—in the form of a six-pound baby. God's entrusted me with a life, a little soul that never was before, and I have to do my best to love and raise him into a productive human being."

Izzy rolled his head to one side to look at Mrs. Oakland. "I never thought much about life—or death—until we started researching this story. Now it seems like everything I see or do reminds me of one or the other."

"That's growing up, Izzy. It's a dirty job, but everybody's got to do it."

The big boy grinned and pushed away from the window. "When Franklin James gets big enough to want to toss around a football, call me. I can give him a few pointers."

They left the hospital in silence, consumed by private thoughts. Darby and Jake were surprised when Izzy pulled the car into the lot of the Walters Family Restaurant.

"What are we doing here?"

"I'm hungry. Besides, Molly was spazzing out last time I saw her."

"What's her problem?" Jake asked.

"Blake."

"What now?"

"Blake's decided April Hennessy is the girl for him." Izzy punched open the door. "Molly's really bummed about it. I want to see how she's doing."

Sometimes Izzy surprised her. Darby had always known he was a gentle giant, but even she hadn't realized how concerned Izzy was about Molly. Unless . . . Darby shook her head to clear it. Izzy and Molly? Could it be that Izzy had a crush on Molly? No way. Well, maybe . . .

They sat in Molly's section and she came to them shortly, a wide smile on her face. "Hi. Mr. Walters is out, so I can be friendly. What do you want? There's fresh apple pie."

Molly looked more relaxed today. Something had changed. It only took a moment for Molly to tell them what it was.

"I've got great news!" she announced. "I'm working on a second story for *Live!* I'm doing an article for the Brentwood *Gazette*."

"Without us?" Izzy looked hurt.

"I didn't think you'd be interested. I okayed it with Ms. Wright. She thought my idea was great."

"Are you going to tell us what it is?"

"A teen makeover! Gary is going to do 'before' and 'after' shots. It will be one of those 'ugly-duckling-turned-beautiful-swan' stories. Women love those sorts of stories."

"And who, if I may ask, is your 'ugly duckling'?"

"Me, of course!"

"You?" Jake questioned. "But you aren't an ugly duckling!"

"*Something* must be wrong with me."

"Because Blake dumped you? I think not."

"Don't try to make me feel better, Izz. He dropped me. Splat. Just like that. I must have done *something* wrong!"

Darby stared at Molly in disbelief. Molly Ashton was one of the most attractive girls at Brentwood High. A little ditzy, yes. Ugly? Never. "You've got this all wrong, Molly."

"Never mind. I'm doing it. Ms. Wright thought it would be a fun, light piece, so you might as well save your breath. And . . ." Molly's eyes narrowed and a look of fierce determination crossed her features, ". . . when I'm done, Blake Denton is going to eat his heart out." She blinked and the fierceness was replaced by Molly's usual sunny expression. "So, do you want pie or not?"

"Molly's nuts!" Izzy yelped when they returned to his vehicle.

"She's hurting, that's all. She's trying to find a way to get back at Blake."

"That's crazy. If he can't see what a good thing he had in Molly, that's *his* problem. She shouldn't go changing herself for a guy. She's fine the way she is."

"At least she's doing it for a story," Jake commented. "Ms. Wright will keep an eye on her. Nothing can go wrong."

"Unless she decides to dye her hair black," Darby muttered, remembering their conversation about April Hennessy.

Izzy groaned.

"I'll talk to Sarah," Darby offered. "She's got a great head on her shoulders. Between us, we can keep Molly in line . . . I think."

"Sarah." Izzy latched onto the name like a drowning man to a life raft. "She can handle Molly. She's great."

"She is, isn't she?" Jake added. "I'm glad she's on our team—it's good to get to know her."

"I think she's been pretty left out of things," Darby said. "The wheelchair and all."

"It is weird, having to look down at her all the time and having that thing wrapped around her. It's too bad. I'll bet a lot of kids never take the time to know her because they feel uncomfortable."

"I'm guilty," Darby admitted, "but that's going to change. There's something really special about Sarah and I can't quite put my finger on it yet."

"It's the church stuff," Izzy said unexpectedly. "That's the difference."

"What do you mean?"

"Sarah's a Christian. That's why she is the way she is. She told me that once. She said she never would have made it this far if she hadn't had God to help her along the way."

"How come you know so much about Sarah?" Jake asked.

"I know about everybody," Izzy retorted cheerfully. "I'm a social kind of guy."

"Then what do you know about Shane Donahue?"

Izzy whistled through his teeth. "You've got me there. Shane's got a mystique just like James Dean did. Shane keeps to himself. Frankly, I don't know much more about Shane than his name."

"Maybe we'll find out now that we're going to be working together," Darby suggested.

"Don't count on it. Shane keeps to himself."

Darby didn't say any more, but she tucked the thought away in her mind. She loved a mystery and Shane Donahue appeared to be one.

CHAPTER 7

LIVE
FROM BRENTWOOD HIGH

"Duffy's Nut House and Dance Studio. Walnuts and wallflowers are our specialty."

"Quit goofing around, Izzy!"

"Hi, Darby. I thought you were my parole officer."

"Very funny. Does your mother know how you answer the phone?"

"Sure. I answer it just like she does."

"You're certifiably crazy. There's no doubt in my mind."

"Is that what you called to tell me?"

"Not exactly. I lined up an interview with Grady O'Brien. He's on call tonight, so he can't come into the city, but he's invited us to his house in Braddington."

"What if he gets a call while we're talking to him?"

"Then we'll have to try again later."

"I guess we'd better do it. Ms. Wright's breathing down our necks as it is. Jake is here right now. I'll pry him out of the refrigerator and we'll be over. Watch for us."

———

"The trip to Braddington seems longer tonight,"

Jake commented as the landscape of the city gave way to fields and rolling hills.

"It must be weird to live in the country." Izzy's gaze scanned the open spaces growing larger and longer as they left the city behind. "Boring. What do people *do* out here?"

"You sound like Andrew Tremaine," Darby pointed out. "And that's *not* a compliment."

"All I'm saying is that I'd be bored. No malls, no multiplex cinemas, no teen clubs, no nothing."

"It's not so bad," Jake said. "I used to live in the country and I liked it."

"You? You're kidding!"

"Don't look at me like I'm an alien who just landed. Just because I don't happen to look like *your* idea of a farm kid—which probably involves bib overalls and hay growing out of my pockets—doesn't mean I don't understand what it's like to grow up in the country."

"So what's it like?"

"Fine. Fun."

"But what did you do?"

"Shot hoops, hung out with my friends, went fishing."

"Bo-ring!"

"Pay no attention to him, Jake," Darby interrupted. "He's trying to act like Andrew."

"And doing a pretty good job!"

Izzy pulled up to a big gray house with black trim and a ruby red front door. "This is it."

Braddington was a clean little town with wide paved streets and big old trees that formed a lush green arch over the street. "Nice," Darby commented.

"Well, what are we waiting for?" Izzy plucked his

notebook off the front seat of the car and wrestled open the door. He sauntered up the sidewalk to the step and hammer-fisted the door.

On the third powerful rap, the door swung open. Grady stood framed in the doorway, a sandwich in one hand, the TV remote in the other. His dark blond hair was slightly mussed. He wore jeans and a white T-shirt. Over the T-shirt was a plaid, hooded shirt, open to the waist. His build was sturdy and solid, like that of an athlete. For all of that, Grady still looked very young. Too young to know how to save lives or to deliver babies.

"Come inside. I'm glad you're here."

"You are?"

Grady grinned and two deep, masculine dimples slashed his cheeks. "Sure. The television cable is on the fritz and we can only get two channels. I was dreading a night on call with nothing to do. Want a soda?"

Grady served sodas and dumped peanuts and pretzels into dishes on the coffee table in the living room before launching himself backward into a brown and beige plaid recliner.

"So, what do you want to know?"

"Everything."

"That should be easy. I was born at the Braddington Hospital eighteen years ago in June. My father, John, and mother, Mary, were delighted to have a son to carry on the family name. . . . Would you like me to tell about all my adventures as a toddler or skip right into first grade?"

"I think I should qualify my question." Izzy kicked off his shoes to make himself more comfortable. "I want to know everything about the emergency medical technician program."

"It's not as interesting as my life story," Grady warned cheerfully, "but I can give you a rundown. Every year more than a hundred thousand people die unnecessarily in our country due to a lack of emergency medical services. Many people could be saved who die from heart attacks, overdoses, car and bike accidents, and the like."

"Then why aren't they?"

"Good question. I asked the same thing myself. When I heard that it was because of a lack of emergency services, I decided that the best thing I could do about it was to become a volunteer. Here in Braddington, the EMT program was having a hard time recruiting volunteers. A lot of people have their family physicians in the city, so our hospital has to struggle all the time. Still, if you've fallen and broken an arm or leg or have a child who is bleeding profusely from a head wound, an hour's drive to the city for medical help can be a long, long time. That's why it's important to maintain hospitals in rural communities. When I heard that I could become an EMT at eighteen, I thanked my mother for not starting me in school until I was over six years old, and I signed up. It seemed to me that if I could just help to save *one life*, all the work would be worth it."

Izzy looked toward the window. "Braddington's pretty quiet. Do you have much 'business'?"

"More than we'd like to have. Farm accidents are a big problem out here. And anywhere there's a highway, there are traffic accidents. After all, there are close to a million and a half highway injuries every year. Braddington gets its share."

Jake whistled through his teeth. "I never realized . . ."

"Most people don't. It's pretty easy to think you're invincible, that nothing will ever hurt you, that bad things only happen to someone else. The first thing I learned on this job was that that kind of 'magical thinking' was false. *Anyone* can have an accident, be burned, or get sick." Grady's eyes grew troubled. "You grow up fast on this job."

"What *is* your job, exactly?"

"EMTs are an extension of the hospital emergency room. When patients can't come to the hospital, we take the care to them. We identify the problems, do what treatment we can, and bring them back to the hospital for further treatment."

"And sometimes you even deliver babies!"

"Yep! My goal has always been to become a doctor. The experiences I've had as an EMT have made me more certain than ever that I've made the right choice. I've learned how important it is to believe in myself and what I do and to keep on learning and growing. I couldn't live with myself if I ever thought I was offering our patients anything but the best I can be. But don't think that every time we get a call there's a baby on the way. Mrs. Oakland was my first.

"Usually our job involves stopping hemorrhages, treating shock, and keeping broken bones in place until we can get a patient to the hospital."

Izzy cleared his throat and poised his pen over the notebook resting on the arm of his chair. "Who shows you how to do all this?"

"There's a class—over a hundred hours of train-ing—which all EMTs must take." Grady grinned. "And it helps to have a strong stomach and a level head."

"What is *that* supposed to mean?" Izzy said suspi-ciously, as though he wasn't sure he wanted to hear the answer.

"Last month we were called to a farm accident. A limb had been severed and was still caught in the piece of farm machinery. Not only did we have to stop the hemorrhaging at the site of the amputation we had to disentangle the limb and get it on ice so that the doc-tors had the possibility of reattachment. And once we were called to transport an animal-bite victim. Have you ever seen what teeth can do to a face—"

Grady stopped short and leaned forward. "Your color isn't good, Izzy. Are you sure *you're* feeling okay?"

"I *was*, until you started to talk." Izzy's voice trem-bled. "If we could just change the subject. . . ."

"Sure," Grady agreed cheerfully. "Want to see my beeper?" He unclipped the small black box from his belt and handed it to Izzy. "As soon as it beeps, I go to the hospital immediately. That's why I was glad you agreed to drive out tonight. It gets pretty boring hang-ing around home waiting for that thing to—"

A loud, piercing noise split the air.

"Guess I spoke too soon. Can we finish this later?" Grady shrugged off the laid-back teenaged-boy image he'd been projecting. He became brisk and business-like, his manner and movements precise.

They followed Grady to the driveway of his house. Izzy dug in the pocket of his jeans for a key. "I'll move my car so you can back out."

"Just give me a ride to the hospital. It will be faster. I can walk home later." Without waiting for assent, Grady slid into the front seat of the car.

"How fast can I go?" Izzy hunkered down in front of the steering wheel, itching for a race.

"The speed limit. We don't need to cause an accident on the way to one."

"Is that what being an EMT makes you? Responsible? *Adult?*" Izzy sounded disappointed.

"It has to happen sooner or later," Grady said lightly. "Turn here. Drop me off at the first door. Thanks for the ride."

They watched as he disappeared into the hospital through doors marked "EMERGENCY ROOM ENTRANCE." Moments later, a large door opened and the Braddington ambulance pulled out, its lights already flashing.

"Impressive," Jake said as the vehicle disappeared from sight. "That guy makes me feel like I've been wasting my life or something."

"Maybe that's the angle for our story!" Darby exclaimed. "Teenagers *do* waste a lot of time. Rural hospitals are short of volunteers. Maybe our story will influence kids who might be interested in medicine as a career to take a look at the EMT program."

"You're too optimistic," Izzy growled. "You seem to think we can pull a story together with the little scraps of information we have so far." Izzy's eyes narrowed and his forehead furrowed in thought. "Unless . . ."

Without warning, Izzy shifted the car into gear and bore down on the gas pedal. Darby was caught by surprise and fell against Jake as the car careened onto the highway.

"Izz! What do you think you're doing?"

"Slow down, buddy."

"Can't. I want to catch up with the ambulance." Izzy's knuckles whitened around the steering wheel as he increased his speed.

"Have you lost your mind?"

"Stop it, Izz. We can't do this!"

"Why not? This is research. I wish we had a camera. We'd probably get some great footage."

Darby recognized the determination on her friend's face. For as long as she'd known Isador Eugene Mooney, she'd known the signs of trouble. He'd worn that expression the time he'd insisted his parents *wanted* him to invite thirty children for supper the evening of his eighth birthday. He'd worn it again when he'd decided that he and Darby should sabotage the upperclassmen's Homecoming float. If she hadn't put her foot down, Izzy would have gotten them both suspended.

With a sinking feeling in the pit of her stomach, Darby pleaded, "Don't be stupid! We can't chase the ambulance!"

"Who says I'm chasing an ambulance? This is a free country. I can drive down this road if I want. . . . There it is!" In the distance was a winking red glow of lights.

Amid protests from Darby and Jake, Izzy pulled within a few yards of another car parked on the side road. Several people were milling about. A truck sat at a skewed angle, half in and half out of the ditch.

"What's happening?" Izzy asked one of the spectators.

"Ben Furman's hired man had a bit too much to drink in town. Drove into the ditch. He's just lucky he didn't tip the truck over. He could have killed himself."

"Was he hurt?"

"Doesn't look like it." The man pointed to a fellow dressed in denim work clothes leaning against the truck. Grady and the other members of the ambulance crew were with him. "We thought we'd better call the ambulance, though. Better to be safe than sorry. The thing that's probably going to hurt the worst is getting his license taken away. Serves him right, though. Nobody has any business drinking and driving . . . wha. . . ?"

At the change in the man's voice, Darby spun around. A sudden flurry of activity had erupted near the truck. The man in denim, who'd been gesticulating wildly with his arms, had sunk to the ground. The EMTs huddled over him.

"Arthur must have had a heart attack!" the gentleman next to Darby exclaimed.

"Oh, oh," Izzy muttered. "Oh, oh, oh . . ."

"I don't know what we'd do without ambulance service out here. They've saved so many lives. . . ."

"What are they doing to him?" Izzy wondered aloud. First, Grady tapped the man as if to get his attention and spoke loudly in his ear. When the man didn't respond, Grady rubbed his knuckles along the man's chest. Still no response. Quickly, the EMTs moved the patient to his back, and Grady tilted the victim's head backward, putting one hand on the man's forehead, the other near his chin. Grady leaned close to the fellow's mouth, as if listening for the sound of breathing.

Grady must have heard nothing, for immediately he and his partner began cardiopulmonary resuscitation.

"CPR," the older man next to them blurted. "I'm

taking a class myself. It's exhausting work. Lots of ways to make mistakes too."

"Mistakes?" Darby's voice was shaky. "What do you mean?"

"Not giving full breaths, not having the victim's head tipped back far enough, not getting a good seal around the patient's mouth . . . lots of things."

Darby could see a T-shaped patch of sweat plastering Grady's shirt to his back as he worked. He held a man's life in his hands, Darby realized. No wonder he was sweating. She'd be sweating too.

Because Darby and Jake's attention was riveted on the dramatic scene before them, it was several minutes before they turned around to look for Izzy. They found him fainted dead away, in a crumpled heap on the grass behind them.

CHAPTER **8**

LIVE

FROM BRENTWOOD HIGH

"Feeling better?"

Izzy's eyes fluttered open. "What happened?"

"You fainted."

Izzy rolled his head to one side and groaned.

"We know one thing for sure. You'll never make it in the medical field. You don't even have to see blood to pass out."

"Where are we?"

"On the way back to Brentwood. Grady was tied up and we wanted to get out of there."

"How'd I get into the car?" Izzy ran his hands over the stubble of his hair. He blinked owlishly to focus his eyes.

"Brute strength. Darby's got more muscle than any other girl I know."

"You *lifted* me into the car?"

"That man we were talking to helped us."

"Actually, he wanted the EMTs to take a look at you too, but I convinced him that you did this all the time. You *are* okay, aren't you?"

"Everything but my pride. That's been mortally wounded. I should never have followed that ambulance." Izzy crossed his arms belligerently across his chest and scowled. "And I should never have signed up for this program."

"Don't be silly. You're perfect for *Live! From Brentwood High*. You'll go to any lengths to get a story. That's what real reporters do."

"But they don't pass out when they finally find it."

"He's really something, isn't he?" Darby murmured, more to herself than to the others.

"Who? Izzy? He certainly is. What, I'm not sure, but definitely 'something'!"

"Not Izz. Grady! He's *awesome*. So mature."

"Did he impress you *that* much?"

"I didn't realize how cool and collected he'd be under pressure. Some people *talk* about saving lives, but he goes out and *does* it!"

This story was taking on real significance for Darby. It was no longer simply an exercise in information gathering. It had become *real*. Someone not many months older than herself was involved in life or death issues. The idea made Darby feel very young and ineffective, but *Live! From Brentwood High* gave her the tools to make a change. Even though she might not be able to be an EMT herself, she could tell the story to others. Who could know how many teenagers might become interested in emergency medical services as a result of their feature?

"You guys have all the fun!" Molly blurted when Team One met to compile their research the next afternoon. The aroma of chocolate-almond coffee was wafting through the air of Cafe Espresso. "All we did was bookwork. I must have a million statistics on heart attack and burn victims, Good Samaritan laws, and the legal obligations of EMTs. You got to see the real thing!"

"Be grateful." Andrew looked up from his cup of cappuccino. "At least we didn't have to drive all the way into the sticks to interview Wonder Boy."

"That reminds me," Jake said, ignoring Andrew's foul mood, "we *do* have to talk to Grady again tonight. He got called away before we finished asking him the questions we'd prepared."

"Count me out," Andrew said. "I'm allergic to all that fresh air."

"I've got to work at the restaurant tonight. One of the waitresses asked me to sub for her. Mr. Walters must have gotten to be too much for her. She said she needed a night off."

"And I'm volunteering at the nursing home," Sarah said. "We're having a sing-along."

"Guess that leaves us," Jake commented. "Right Darby? Izz?"

"I've got stuff to do." Izzy's cheeks turned a ruddy pink. "I can't go."

"Can't go or *won't* go?" Andrew prodded. "Maybe you're embarrassed to see this Grady fellow—just in case he noticed your big fainting act."

Izzy glared at Andrew. If looks could kill, Andrew would have been long gone.

"It's okay." Sarah reached across the table and patted Izzy's hand. "He probably didn't see a thing. And if he did, it's no big deal. Grady sounds like a really great guy. He won't hold it against you."

Leave it to Sarah to smooth ruffled feathers. Izzy's broad shoulders relaxed. Just as Andrew always knew exactly the *wrong* thing to say, Sarah seemed to know the right. The ruddy color even began to seep out of Izzy's cheeks.

"I guess I could go. Just don't let me follow any more ambulance calls."

————

Grady was waiting for them in the front yard. He was sprawled in a hammock that sagged nearly to the ground, listening to headphones and tapping out a rhythm with the toe of one shoe. A big German Shepherd lay beneath the hammock, contentedly wagging his tail back and forth in a fanlike motion.

"Hard work being an EMT," Jake commented as he neared the pair.

Grady opened one eye and grinned. "I'm resting up. I know you have questions." He looked inquiringly at Izzy. "Are you all right? Yesterday I saw some commotion around you out of the corner of my eye, but when I looked again, you were gone."

"Fine. Great. Nothing. Not a thing. Nope. Not me. . . ."

Darby and Jake both burst out laughing, leaving Grady looking a little puzzled. "So then, let's get to it." Grady swung the hammock and the Shepherd scrambled out of the way. "What are your questions?"

"What's the *hardest* thing about being an EMT?"

Grady settled deeper into the hammock and stared at the sky through the canopy of dark green leaves. "I guess it's the death thing."

"The 'death thing'?"

"Sure. You know. Having people die. Not being able to help them. Doing everything in your power to save someone and failing. That's definitely the hardest."

"That's happened to you?" Izzy whispered.

"On my third call. I wasn't expecting it and I wasn't prepared. I thought we were going to a heart-attack victim. They didn't tell us that the family had found him in the garage and didn't know cardiopulmonary resuscitation. When the call came, it was already too late. It only takes four to six minutes without oxygen for the brain cells to begin to die."

Grady dropped a tennis-shoe-clad foot over the side of the hammock. He looked very young and very old all at the same moment.

"You don't know what to expect . . . the first time you see a dead body, I mean. It's especially difficult if the patient has been having respiratory difficulty, because the skin turns different colors and . . ."

Izzy grew very pale.

"Do you want me to stop?"

Softhearted, weak-stomached Izzy clamped his lips more tightly together and shook his head.

"I thought I was prepared," Grady continued, "but nothing really prepares you for that. It's incredible, really, how your training takes over and you just do what you have to do without thinking about it. Then later, when the crisis is past, you wonder, Did I actually *do* that? Did I follow all the procedures when my brain and my feelings felt totally turned off?"

"How *can* you handle it? I mean, a dead person . . ." Izzy's voice trailed away.

"I've learned to think of death as a part of life. One more step on the continuum. Difficult as it is to accept, it's normal. Sometimes it's expected. In situations like that, it's as important for us to be there for the survivors as for the victim." Grady sighed. "Still, it's much harder than I thought it would be."

"Then why do you do it?"

"Because it's my dream. For a long time I thought that being a doctor was . . . well, glamorous . . . like being a movie star or something." A wry smile slipped across Grady's features. "I figured out how foolish that idea was soon enough. There's nothing enviable about the responsibility doctors carry. But it made me more sure than ever that that's what I want to be. The EMT program is just one small step toward my dream."

"You couldn't pay me enough to do what you do!" The color still had not returned to Izzy's cheeks. "And you do it for free!"

"I don't care about the money. The experience is enough—that and the fact that I can be there for the people who need help."

"I don't think that would be enough to get me to do what you do. Blood, open wounds, needles . . . no thanks. Not me!"

"We're trained to work in less than perfect conditions. It would be unrealistic to expect anything else. If everything were under control, we wouldn't be needed."

"Let's say you're called to the scene of an accident. What's first?"

"Several things go on at once. We have to make sure that the scene is secure, evaluate and treat the patient, then package and transport him or her to the hospital."

"Package? Sounds like you're boxing cookies or wrapping loaves of bread!"

"That just means getting the patient ready to be moved."

"Don't you just put a person on a stretcher? That's the way they do it on TV."

"Television is a sanitized version of what we do."

"It's messy enough for me."

Grady looked at Izzy sympathetically. "Not everyone is cut out for this type of work. I wondered about my own capabilities for a long time after I learned about *triage*."

"Tree-ahhh-what?"

"*Triage*. It's a French word that means 'picking' or 'sorting.' If we have several patients to attend to, it's the way we decide which person will be treated first, second, and so on."

"Isn't that a little like deciding who'll live and who'll die?"

"In a way, yes. That really bugged me for a long time. I didn't want to play God. Finally one of my instructors got it through my head that triage was a way of saving lives, not losing them."

"Explain."

"It's a method of classifying patients according to the seriousness of their injuries. Once they began to use it in the Korean War, many more of the injured survived."

"Why?"

"By making our first priority those who are most severely injured but who still have a good chance at survival, and our second priority those who can wait for transport."

"So what's your *third* priority?"

"Broken bones, of course, and other injuries that can wait." Grady's expression tightened. "And those with whom death seems certain."

"Oh, man . . ." Izzy's broad, compassionate face crumpled. "I couldn't do it. No way, no how."

"It sounds tough, I know. It *is* tough. I've never been a triage officer—that's always the most experienced EMT."

"So if you're left at the scene of an accident while others are being put into the ambulance, that means one of two things," Izzy deduced. "You're either not hurt too badly and can be moved later because they know you'll make it, or . . . it's already too late."

"This is totally depressing!" Darby blurted. "How can you stand it?"

"You're not hearing what I'm saying," Grady pointed out softly. "You keep thinking about losing lives. I'm thinking about *saving* them. Without well-trained emergency personnel, *more* people wouldn't make it."

"I think I get it." Izzy smacked the eraser tip of his pencil on the table. "My mom used to put a glass on the table and pour water into it. Then she'd say, 'Isador, is this glass half full or half empty?' I'd look at it for a long time, not being able to decide. See, the glass was *both*. It just depended on whether I wanted to see things in a positive or a negative light. We're saying the glass is half empty. Grady says it's half full! Just because you can't save everybody doesn't mean it's not important to save all the people you can."

Izzy folded his arms across his chest and smiled with an air of superiority.

"That's the first time I've heard it put quite that way, Izzy, but you're right. I think about the people I can help, not those I can't. Frankly, it's one of the greatest feelings in the world to know that I can actually make a difference to someone."

"But if someone *dies* . . ."

"There are some things I had to accept when I started working. One was that death does happen. Sometimes it happens on my calls. The second thing I had to accept was that it is *not my fault*. It's scary, yes. I cried. A lot. I learned that it's not something I could push down inside of myself and ignore. My parents have been great about being there for me, for listening. But, eventually, I realized that what I do allows people to live who might otherwise have died. I'll never totally accept the death thing, but at least I'm learning to put it into perspective."

Grady chuckled at the expression on Izzy's face. "I know this will probably blow you away, but there's something really *exciting* about this job—never knowing what we're going to find when we reach our destination, never knowing what it is we're walking into. There's kind of a rush with that. My adrenalin is pumping. I'm psyched. It's hard to explain, but it's important that you understand. Working as an EMT has reaffirmed what it is that I want to do with my life. There's a satisfaction in it that money can't buy. It *feels* right. I've treated human life—and won. Every one of the patients I've handled stays with me. I'll never forget them. Those calls are like big exclamation points in my mind."

"I'm glad you can handle it," Izzy muttered. "I couldn't. If someone just kept screaming and screaming and screaming . . ."

"You block it. You do what you've been trained to do. You keep talking to the patient, calming, soothing.

Still, the more experienced EMTs say that there's always going to be one you can't handle."

"What do you do then?"

"Walk away and pull yourself together. Sometimes I've found that I'm fine at the accident—and sick when I get home.

"I've been lucky. I haven't had many rough experiences. Although I spent the longest twenty minutes of my life doing CPR on a patient while whipping down the highway at ninety miles an hour . . . Izzy, you don't look very well. Are you all right?"

Izzy groaned. Darby and Jake spun to face him. "Don't faint!" they chimed together.

Even Izzy, whose complexion had turned a familiar shade of gray, had to join Grady's burst of surprised laughter.

CHAPTER 9

LIVE

FROM BRENTWOOD HIGH

"What great luck!" Jake exclaimed as they drove through Brentwood the next evening, still discussing the interview they'd had with Grady the previous day.

"I don't see what you're so excited about." Izzy examined his fingernails with exaggerated care. "No big deal."

"*No big deal?* Izz, this is a humongous deal! Don't you get it? Our story is shaping up. I can see it now . . ." Jake gestured as he paused at a stoplight. "We'll start with a big bang intro—something like an ambulance roaring down a country road or the EMTs at work. We'll have to be careful that we don't show any faces— the privacy factor and all. From there we can go to the body of the piece and get the story out about what teenage volunteers are doing in the rural areas. It will be a great balance to all the negative stories about teenage gangs and violence. We can close with a great quote by Grady . . ."

"Anybody hungry?"

"Izzy, don't you even *care* about this project?"

"Sure I do, but I care about my stomach more. Hey! There's Sarah's van. Turn in here."

With a sigh, Jake followed Izzy's pointing finger and

pulled up next to the burgundy van in the fast-food restaurant's parking lot. Izzy scrambled out of the car.

"What are you doing here?" Molly blurted as the threesome trooped into line behind them.

"Bumming around; talking about our interview with Grady O'Brien in Braddington. We've all missed supper. Who wants a burger?"

Jake and Darby left Izzy and Molly in charge of buying food to join Sarah at a booth at the far end of the dining area.

"Can we all fit in here?" Darby asked.

"Sure. You and Jake take one side, Molly and Izzy can have the other. I'll just roll up to the end of the table. Oops! I forgot to get ketchup."

"Stay here. I'll get it."

While Jake was gone, Sarah turned to Darby. "Well, how was it?"

"Good. Jake's really enthusiastic. Izzy's a little less sure about the whole story."

"Don't pay any attention to Izzy. The whole idea of doing research about medical things bothers him. You'll have to work around him just like Molly and I had to work around Andrew today."

"Did I hear you say the name of that lazy slug Andrew Tremaine?" Molly slapped a tray of food onto the table. The humidity had turned her always curly hair into a halo of frizz. There was a high color in her cheeks and her eyes flashed with irritation. "Please don't mention his name now. I want to eat. Andrew is bad for my digestion."

"You mean he makes you sick to your stomach," Izzy interpreted as he approached the table with another trayload of food. "Me too."

"This must be serious," Jake commented lazily, "if it's bad enough to ruin Izzy's appetite."

"Oh, he's not so bad," Sarah protested.

"That's just like you, Sarah, to try to see the best in people." As she spoke Molly dealt out burgers and fries with a practiced hand. "Unfortunately, there is no 'best' in Andrew."

"What did he do now?" Darby poked a french fry into the little cup of ketchup Izzy set in front of her.

"Nothing. Absolutely nothing. Except whine. And complain. And nitpick, criticize, nag, grumble, and fuss."

"Sorry I missed this," Jake said with an insincere grin. "Sounds like you had all the fun."

"He knew perfectly well that we were supposed to be researching the EMT program. I even found the material he needed and set it in front of him! But did he read it? Oh, no; no way. Instead he wandered around the library making passes at all the girls and stealing pencils from the tables near the card catalogue computers. He's totally childish and self-absorbed."

"How does he expect to get credit if all he does is goof off?"

"I don't think he cares. He says that guys like Grady are wasting their time. Andrew thinks he's *immortal* or something. He refuses to consider that someday even *he* might get hurt or sick and need help. He thinks that nothing is ever going to 'get' him. Andrew says that people who get hurt or sick are just weak, and if they'd been more careful, nothing would have happened to them."

"Nice guy." Darby dumped her ketchup onto the hamburger wrapper and sprinkled it with salt and pepper. Thoughtfully she dragged a greasy fry through the red puddle. "Ms. Wright said that our groups would be smaller for the next assignment. Maybe Andrew will decide he doesn't want to work with us anymore."

"I hope so." Molly crumpled a paper napkin in her fist. "Andrew's been trying to get me to go out with him for weeks. As if I'd want to . . . even to make Blake jealous."

Her expression turned pensive. "Too bad his personality isn't as cute as his face." Her eyes grew wide. "I can't believe I said that! 'Andrew' and 'cute' in the same sentence! Yuk!"

"He's a first-class jerk," Izzy pronounced. Then he stuffed most of a bacon-cheeseburger into his mouth. As he chewed, his cheeks puffed out like a squirrel with a mouthful of nuts. "He doesn't care about the story."

"Or about us," Molly added. "I want this story to be absolutely perfect. How many high-school students actually get to produce a television feature for the ten o'clock news? I don't want to be embarrassed because a guy like Andrew didn't pull his own weight."

Sarah gently cleared her throat, obviously uncomfortable with the path this conversation had taken. Sarah was rarely critical of anyone—even the likes of Andrew Tremaine.

"Tell us about your visit to the country," Sarah urged. "What did Grady have to say?"

When they were done relating the details of their interview with Grady, Molly stamped her foot beneath the table. "No fair! Next time I'm going to do the interview, and one of you can go to the library with Andrew."

"Me too," Sarah added wistfully. "Even though Andrew wasn't hitting on me every fifteen minutes, I wasn't crazy about the library either."

"Next time we want to be in on the excitement!"

"Then why don't you come with me tonight?" Izzy startled them all. He'd been quietly stuffing onion rings into his mouth and listening to the others talk.

"Grady told me that there is an EMT class being held in Brentwood right now," Izzy said around his food. "He said that if any of us wanted to attend, he'd make arrangements with the instructor. It's the same instructor who trained him. I told him some of us would be there."

"Great!" Molly gathered together the litter of scrap paper around her seat. "Let's go. I'll call Mom and tell her I won't be home till later. How about it, Sarah?"

"I'm sure it will be fine with my parents. They're really excited about my getting involved in this program."

"It's all set then. Let's go."

"Guess you'll have to ride with me." Sarah patted the armrest on her chair. "I'm hard to fit into a two-seater."

Izzy, Molly, and Sarah disappeared in a flurry of excitement.

"Whew!" Darby sat back in the booth with a relieved sigh. "I'm glad that's settled."

"Did you want to go with them?" Jake asked.

"No. Molly's right. It will be good for her and Sarah to do this. Besides, I have tons of homework to finish tonight."

"Me too." Jake stared at her, his gray-green eyes hooded by the long, dusky fringe of his lashes.

As the long silence between them grew, Darby felt

a strange restlessness overtake her. She was painfully aware of Jake's eyes upon her and of the way his sandy blond hair feathered back over his ears and curved around the nape of his neck.

Jake Saunders had to be one of the best-looking guys at Brentwood—and here he was, sitting across the table from her, watching her as though she were the most important person in the entire world. Her insides did a lurch—the same kind they did when she rode Thunder Peak, the roller coaster in the amusement park at the edge of the city.

"You've got a strange look on your face," Jake commented with a smile.

Darby realized for the first time that his gray-green eyes were flecked with a darker color, almost emerald.

"Something wrong?"

Not a thing. Darby mentally scrambled to pull herself together. *What's wrong with me? I practically watched the birth of a baby with this guy, and now I can't think of anything to say!*

"Darby?"

"Sorry. I'm zoning out. Overload, maybe."

"Me too. I didn't realize how involved I'd become in the story. I thought *Live! From Brentwood High* was going to be like another school class—boring and routine. But this is different. It's *real.* Grady is my age and helping to save lives. Makes me think I've been wasting my life!"

"Grady's an exception."

"Maybe, but there's no reason that you and I can't be 'exceptions' too. Maybe we're expecting too little of ourselves. Newspapers are full of things teenagers have done wrong—car theft, robbery, vandalism. We can't blame anyone but ourselves if adults think teenagers are irresponsible or lazy. With *Live!* we have a chance to talk about teens who are doing something positive. I'd like to think I could be one of them."

Darby was beginning to understand why she was so attracted to Jake. His looks didn't hurt, but there was more—a steadiness, a maturity, a compassion, that made her feel secure when she was around him. Instinctively Darby *trusted* Jake.

"You're doing it again."

She met his eyes guiltily. "Doing what?"

"Zoning out. *What* are you thinking about?"

My crush on you. Is that what you want to hear?

Darby waved her hand in front of her face, hoping that one of Jake's many abilities wasn't mind reading. "Maybe we should go. My parents are expecting me home."

With one last longing look at those gray-green eyes and endless lashes, Darby gathered her school books from the seat beside her.

"I'll give you a ride. Come on."

When Jake's fingers touched her elbow, Darby could have sworn that zingers of electricity danced up her arm. She bit her lip to hide the grin that threatened, composed her expression, and turned to him. "Great. Let's go."

———

The Ellison house was a modern split-level located in a tract of new housing on the east edge of Brentwood. The house, white, with gray trim and a big red double front door, looked inviting beneath the street lights.

"Can you come inside for a minute? If I introduce you to my mom she's less apt to give me a lecture for being late."

"And who's going to get *me* out of trouble?" A lazy smile spread across Jake's face. "Sure, why not? I'll be your hero, riding on a white horse to rescue you from your nasty jailer."

"I wouldn't recommend telling Mom that's why you're here. She's got a great sense of humor, but it only goes so far."

They were laughing as they entered the foyer. Three steps up, in the living room, the lights were lit invitingly. In the family room, several steps down and opposite the formal living room, Darby could hear the television muttering out the news. That meant her father was already home.

"Darb, is that you . . . oh, hi!" Mrs. Ellison appeared in the kitchen doorway, wiping her hands on a dish towel. She was still wearing her white nurse's uniform, but her feet were bare, and her hair, usually worn up for work, had tumbled down her back. Darby was struck with how young her mother looked standing in the doorway, grinning at Jake.

"Mom, this is Jake Saunders. He's in the *Live!* program with me. Sorry we're late."

"It's okay. I just got home. I threw a ham in the oven so it could start cooking while I changed." She smiled and an impish gleam sparkled in her eyes. "I usually don't dress like this to cook."

"You're a nurse?"

"Yes. Right now I'm an office nurse for a surgeon here in Brentwood, but I do miss working in the hospital as well. Perhaps I'll go back after Darby graduates. Now it's nice to be assured I'll be home evenings with her."

"You didn't tell me," Jake accused, turning to Darby.

"I didn't think it mattered."

"Maybe we could use your mom for the story."

"But she's not an EMT."

Mrs. Ellison interrupted the argument. "I think it's really great that you kids are doing something on the rural EMT program. When I was first out of nursing school I worked in a small hospital. So often people who could have been saved got to us too late. Now, with the training and efficiency of the EMTs, many more lives are being saved."

"See! That's a great quote. Can we use it, Mrs. Ellison?"

Nancy Ellison laughed. "Sure. I'm flattered. You didn't think your mother ever said anything quotable, did you, Darb?"

"Motherrrr . . ." Darby moaned, but she smiled. Horribly embarrassing as parents could be, she really didn't mind her own. They were pretty cool . . . considering.

"Now that you've met my quotable mother, you'll probably want to meet my dad too." Shyly Darby reached for Jake's hand and pulled him toward the family room. Out of the corner of her eye, she saw her mother wink at her and give a thumbs-up sign of approval. A flush of pleasure coursed through Darby. It meant a lot that her mother liked Jake.

"I suppose he's a doctor or something."

"Close. A dentist."

"Ouch. Maybe I don't want to meet him."

"He's painless. For years he was a pediatric dentist. His only clients were little kids. Later he decided to become an orthodontist." Darby bared her teeth and clacked them together menacingly. "See his work?"

Darby's father did appear painless enough sprawled across the navy and red plaid couch in the family room. The newspaper was littered all around him, and he was pointing the remote control at the television. "Dumb thing," he muttered. "Dozens of stations and nothing worth watching. Oh, hi, Darby."

"Hi, Dad. There's someone here I'd like you to meet." She planted a kiss on the top of his dark brown head. Her dad always smelled like peppermint, shaving lotion, and antiseptic. Today was no exception. Dr. Ellison had changed into jeans and a flannel shirt. His hair, dark and curly like Darby's, was cut close to his head. Still, some of the more persistent curls had sprung into ringlets near his temples.

When the introductions were complete, Dr. Ellison gestured Jake into the big navy wing chair across from him. "Saunders. That name is very familiar. The contractor who built this house was named Jim Saunders. Any chance you've heard of him?"

"My dad's a contractor, and his name is Jim Saunders. He owns Saunders Construction."

"That's the guy!" Dr. Ellison grinned. "Small world, isn't it? Tell your dad he did a good job on this house. It's the best house we've ever had."

Darby hid her smile as Jake and her father enthusiastically discussed the merits of six-inch insulation and maintenance-free siding. This was easier than she'd expected. Her parents had taken to Jake immediately and vice versa. A tickle of excitement grew within her. *Darby Ellison and Jake Saunders*. Those two names sounded surprisingly nice together. . . .

———

"Can you stay for supper, Jake?" Darby's mom padded barefoot through the family room. She'd changed into jeans and a Harvard sweatshirt and looked more like Darby's twin sister than her mother. "Ham, scalloped potatoes, and chocolate eclairs from that little French bakery on 7th Street."

"We already had a burger, Mom."

"Besides, I wouldn't want to be any bother . . ." Jake looked at Darby for a clue as to what he should do.

"No bother. Let me go open a can of corn and we'll be ready to eat. A hamburger isn't enough for growing teenagers. This will also give us a chance to know Jake. Steve, you and the kids can come up in a few minutes."

This was an amazing stamp of approval from Darby's parents. More amazing still was that *Jake* seemed as comfortable with her parents as they did with him!

Darby settled a little deeper into her chair, her eyes fixed on the television newscaster. Jake did the same. As they silently stared at the screen, Darby felt herself wishing . . . no *willing* . . . the story they were working on to be really special. *Live! From Brentwood High* had opened a door into a new life for Darby, and she was eager to see what she might find on the other side.

"Not that way, Izzy! You do the Heimlich maneuver like this."

Molly hugged Isador around the waist, her elbows held out away from his ribs. She made a fist with one hand and placed her thumb above his navel.

As she grasped her fist with the other hand, Izzy grabbed her hands and pulled them apart.

"Remind me never to invite you to another EMT class."

"How was it?" Jake asked as he and Andrew approached the group. "Did you learn anything?"

"I did." Molly appeared well satisfied with herself. "We covered the Heimlich maneuver and started to learn cardiopulmonary resuscitation. If every adult knew CPR, a lot of lives would be saved. I've signed up for another class. I'm going to learn how to do it."

"Aren't you kind of scrawny to be doing CPR?" Andrew asked. "What if some big fat guy has a heart attack? What good could you do?"

"First of all, I don't appreciate being called scrawny, *Andy*. Besides, my cousin is a lifeguard, and she says it isn't hard at all. I think it would be great to save someone's life." Molly practically glowed at the thought.

"Get real! Why would you want to put your mouth over some stranger's to try to make him breathe?" Andrew sounded genuinely shocked and disgusted. "I wouldn't want a stranger's slobber all over me."

Molly bristled and planted her hands on her hips. She glared daggers at Andrew. "You are the most selfish, inconsiderate, egotistical ... *jerk* ... I have ever met!"

Slowly one of Andrew's eyebrows lifted. The near sneer on his lips became full blown. The look on his face spelled danger. "You're never going to make a difference, Ashton—none of us are—and the sooner you realize that the better. You can spout all this noble stuff about 'helping people' and 'saving the world,' but it's a bunch of baloney. Nobody helps anybody else unless there's a reason—something in it for them. Maybe your friend Grady gets his kicks thinking he's important, but he's not. And the sooner *you* realize that the better. Look out for yourself, Molly. That's what everyone else is doing."

Molly's mouth worked, opening and shutting, without a sound. She turned pale, then flushed pink until everything from the part in her scalp to the base of her neck was suffused with color.

"I think you should withdraw from our program if that's the way you feel. You aren't taking anything we've researched or learned seriously. You don't *care*, and that's going to show up in our report! If you want to preach your negative opinions, go ahead, but do it where I can't hear it. I don't want you dragging the rest of us down with you.

"Why are you in this program anyway?" Molly drilled. "For an easy credit? To sluff off? To get out of class?"

"Back off, Ashton," Andrew said smoothly, surprised by the venom in Molly's words. "So what if I expected this to be easy? That doesn't mean I'm not interested. I see myself as an on-camera personality, that's all. You guys who are good at research can pull it together and—"

"Turn the story over to you to read on the air so you can take all the glory? No thanks, Andrew. You're out of luck. If you don't work behind the scenes, there's no way we're going to let you get in front of a camera!"

"Molly's right, Drew," Izzy said softly. "We're in this together. You can't sit back and slack off and then expect us to let you collect all the praise. We're a *team*. There are six of us to pull the weight for this story, but Ms. Wright said that after the first couple features, we're going to be working in groups of two or three. You aren't going to be able to sit back then. You'll *have* to work. You might as well learn how to do it now."

"Lighten up!" Andrew sputtered, taken aback by the seriousness of the rest of the group. "This isn't a life or death issue, you know!"

"But it *is*. Our first feature is about people who save lives. If we do this right, hundreds of people—maybe thousands—will learn about the rural EMT program. Maybe they'll get donations or volunteers. It's *important*, Andrew, whether you think it is or not."

Izzy stepped between Andrew and Molly. "We're all meeting at my place tonight to put our notes together and eat a pizza. Can you come?" Andrew only glared at

Izzy, but the larger boy ignored the daggered look. "We want you to be there."

"I have a date."

"And that's more important?" Molly questioned in disbelief.

"Bring her along," Jake suggested.

"Great date that would be."

"It's up to you, Drew," Izzy said softly. "But if you don't work on the story, you're out of our group. Everyone pulls their own weight here."

Andrew stared at Izzy in disbelief. "You can't kick me out. Ms. Wright won't let you."

"I have a feeling she might agree with me."

Andrew whipped his jacket off the chair and stormed out. No one spoke as the door to the media room slammed behind him.

Izzy released a long, tense sigh. "Sorry. I probably spoke out of turn."

Sarah maneuvered her wheelchair close to him. "It's okay. He needed to know that we're serious about this project. And he *does* need to be an equal part of the team. We'll stand behind you with Ms. Wright if we need to."

The others nodded in agreement.

"But I don't *want* Andrew to quit." Izzy ran his fingers through his stubbled hair. "I want him to shape up."

"He will now that he knows we're serious," Jake assured him.

"And if he doesn't, do we care?" Molly grumbled. "I know I don't."

"So we just wait and see if he shows up tonight?"

Izzy's expression was dubious. "That should be interesting."

"If you want to talk about *interesting*, listen to this!" Molly pulled a wad of papers out of her purse. "I've made the appointments for my makeover."

"Are you still on that kick?" Izzy frowned at her. "I thought you'd be over it by now."

"I'm doing a story, Isador. You don't 'get over' a story; you get it done."

"I mean about changing yourself into something you aren't, on the off-chance you can make a know-nothing like Blake Denton sorry he dumped you."

"I don't want to talk about Blake."

"Me either. It's *you* we're talking about! Get real, Molly. Blake's the one who needs the makeover, not you."

Molly put her hands over her ears and shook her head. "You just don't understand!"

But they did understand. When would Molly see that changing herself on the *outside* wouldn't make Blake feel or behave any differently on the *inside*?

———

"Is this the right place?" Sarah pulled her van to the curb in front of a small white house in the center of the block in a very ordinary middle-class neighborhood.

"It's not what I expected." Molly stared at the simple but immaculate house. "Of course, I don't know what I *did* expect. Something bigger maybe. This house looks too small for Izzy."

"This place is perfect," Sarah commented as she moved her wheelchair onto the lift. "Not a leaf or a twig anywhere. Looks like they vacuum their yard!"

"When did you two become so interested in lawn care?"

"Not lawn care, exactly," Molly stammered, "but you will have to admit that it's pretty amazing—"

"That a guy who always looks like an unmade bed could live in a house this tidy?"

"Something like that." Molly blushed as Sarah giggled. "Apparently I still have a few things to learn about Isador Mooney." She reached out and punched the doorbell. Almost before it had time to ring, the door glided open. Framed in the doorway were two tiny, doll-like girls.

They were about five years old, petite, and ladylike. The little girls studied Molly, Sarah, and Darby with serious eyes.

"Hi, Darby," the one on the right said as she fingered her long brown braid, then pointed a finger at Sarah and Molly. "Are you my brother's friends, too?" The girls wore identical pink and white dresses, identical bows in their braided hair, and, most amazing, identical contemplative expressions in their brown eyes—Izzy's eyes.

"*Isador*, more company!" The little girl on the left yelled without turning her head. They made no move to leave the doorway or allow the visitors inside. Instead, they stared at Molly and Sarah with undisguised interest, focusing primarily on Sarah's brightly decorated wheelchair.

"Aren't you going to let them in?" Izzy asked as he came to the door. He put a gentle, pawlike hand on each of the girls' heads. The little girls turned in unison to give Izzy adoring smiles.

"They're pretty, Izzy. Which one do you like best?"

A rush of color flooded Izzy's cheeks.

"Izzy's blushing!" one of the twins squealed. The little girls clapped their hands and bounced on their toes, delighted at their big brother's discomfort.

"Get out of here," Izzy ordered gruffly. The tiny pair burst into new gales of laughter.

"Now!"

Giggling, they disappeared into the house, leaving their brother to face the three girls on the steps.

"Little brats," Izzy muttered insincerely.

"They're adorable!" Sarah, with Darby's help, maneuvered her chair into the house. "I didn't know you had sisters."

Izzy mumbled something indistinguishable.

"I'll bet I know why you've kept them a secret," Molly accused. "You didn't want us to know that you had little sisters who could wrap you around their little fingers."

"Hah!" Izzy growled.

"Big, tough Isador Mooney gets gooney about his little sisters!"

"You're way off base, Molly. I hardly ever see the little squirts. . . ."

One of the two pink and white children reappeared and handed Izzy a doll. "Izzy, I can't button the dress on my Barbie. Will you do it for me?"

"I can't right now, Rachel, just wait. . . ."

"But you did Heidi's dolly!" The stamp of a small foot and the threat of imminent tears sent Izzy scurrying to repair the buttons on the tiny dress.

It took all of Darby's willpower not to giggle, seeing her hulking friend bent over a tiny doll that was wearing an evening gown not six inches long. She'd seen the twins before and knew how easily they could charm their older brother.

Izzy looked up at Darby with a glare. "Don't you *dare* laugh."

"I think it's sweet. I didn't know you were so good at playing house."

"Izzy always gets to be the daddy to our dollies," one of the little girls informed their visitors. "He always wants to go to work and leave us alone, but we don't let him. Right, Izzy?"

Izzy's chin was tucked into the collar of his shirt, and his blush had reached the tips of his ears. "There, your dolly is fixed. Now go to your room and play like you promised."

"But Izzy..."

"You *promised*."

Reluctantly the little girls disappeared down the hallway, leaving Izzy to face his friends.

"Don't pay any attention to my little sisters. They're spoiled rotten."

"They're darling, Izz! Like two little dolls."

A grin split Izzy's features. "Yeah, kind of, I guess.... They are pretty great, aren't they?"

"I'm discovering a whole new side of you tonight, Izzy," Sarah said softly. "I like it."

Before he could be embarrassed even further, Izzy ushered them into the living room.

The house was modest but, just as the exterior had been, immaculate. There was a small color television in one corner and across from it sat an elderly, white-haired woman. She was rocking gently in her chair and knitting so swiftly that the needles in her hands seemed to blur.

"Hello, Mrs. Mooney," said Darby cheerfully.

The older woman looked up, and in her eyes was the same sweet expression as that of Izzy's twin sisters. "Well, hello, Darby. Nice to see you again."

"Grandma, I'd like you to meet my friends."

"You children don't want me in here," the older woman said. "I'll just go to my room. . . ."

"It's okay, Grandma. You can stay here. That way you'll be able to hear what we're doing. Right?" Izzy turned expectantly to the others, who immediately nodded an assent. "Grandma lives with us. She helps my mom run a day-care in our house."

"We'd like to have you stay," Sarah said with a smile. "Maybe you'd even have some ideas for us once you hear what we're working on. We can use all the help we can get."

"You children are being very sweet. Of course, I knew you would be—Izzy would have only wonderful friends."

Izzy blushed again, but he leaned over and squeezed his grandmother's hand. When he turned away, Sarah winked at Darby. *We found another soft spot in the big guy*, her look seemed to say.

They had just settled down on the living room floor with notes and papers spread across the carpet when the doorbell rang. Izzy jumped to his feet, in a hurry to get to the door before his little sisters.

"Look who's here!" Jake sauntered into the room with a pouty-looking Andrew in tow.

"Did your date dump you?" Molly asked.

Andrew's expression tightened. "Jake convinced me it would be in my best interests to be here."

"Didn't want to get kicked out of the program, huh?"

"Leave him alone, Molly," Sarah chided. "He's here, isn't he? That's what matters."

"Don't you *ever* get mad at anyone, Sarah?" Molly asked impatiently. "You're even defending *Andrew!*"

"Sure I get angry, but I read something after my accident that I try to remember—'anger resides in the lap of fools.' That's from Ecclesiastes. There was also another thought that kept me patient at a time when all I seemed to do was lose my patience—'be quick to listen, slow to speak and slow to become angry.' Good advice, don't you think?"

"All right, all right!" Molly turned to Andrew. "We're glad you came, no matter *what* Jake had to do to get you here."

"That's better," Sarah said with a chuckle. "But not much."

"It's the best I can do," Molly grumbled. She looked up expectantly as Izzy carried a bowl of chips and a dish of salsa from the kitchen. "Yum! What's this?"

"It's all I could find. Mom's been hiding food from my little sisters again."

"Are you sure it's not *you* she's hiding food from?" Molly poked a finger in the soft roll hanging over Izzy's belt. Izzy sucked in his belly and gave her an indignant glare.

"Help me up, Isador," his grandmother commanded and held out a hand. "I did a little shopping of my own this week. I decided to fill up the candy jar. I bought peppermints, lemon drops, and chocolate kisses. Let me go find them."

After Mrs. Mooney had disappeared into the

kitchen, Jake dropped to the floor beside Darby and Molly. He leaned against the wheel of Sarah's chair. "Tell us what you learned when you researched the EMT program."

"Did you know that half of all heart-attack victims die within two hours?"

"Or that almost ninety percent of poisoning victims are children?"

"That's when emergency medical technicians and ambulance crews can really make a difference because treatment can be started *on the site*. It's the difference between life and death for a lot of patients."

"This is good stuff," Jake murmured as he made notes. "We'll want to get as much of this as possible into the story. Human suffering and drama. Lifesaving teenagers. Great attention draw."

"You're really getting into this, aren't you?"

"I knew I'd like this sort of thing but never realized how much. I wish we had more than ninety seconds for the feature on Channel 9 News. It's a good thing we can have as much time as we need for the uncut version that'll show at school. I'd hate to leave anything out."

"We'll have to condense this to the important stuff."

"But it's *all* important!"

"We can interview Grady with the ambulance in the background."

"Or maybe he'll let us go with him on a call. If we planned it, Gary Richmond could come along and film the whole thing. We could edit it later and do some voice-overs. . . ."

Even Andrew was getting into the spirit of enthusiasm around the project when Izzy's little sisters, now in matching yellow pajamas, came racing into the living room.

"I told you guys to stay in your room while I had company!" Izzy chided.

"Grandma! Grandma!" Rachel yelled.

"She's in the kitchen. Have her wipe your face. You've got chocolate all over it."

"She can't. She's sick!"

Izzy's head snapped upward. "Sick? What do you mean?"

"Her face is a funny color and she's going like this...." Little Rachel put her hands to her throat and began to make a choking sound. Izzy bolted to his feet and raced for the kitchen with Molly and Jake hot on his heels. Darby grasped the handles on Sarah's wheelchair and followed them. Reluctantly Andrew did the same.

The scene in the kitchen was chaos. The candy jar had fallen, and the floor was covered with gumdrops, lemon drops, peppermints, and chocolate kisses. In the middle of this rainbow of sweets was Izzy's grandmother—slumped against the counter. Her face was an alarming bluish gray. Her eyes bulged and her mouth worked but no words came out. She grasped frantically at her throat and with her eyes begged Izzy to do something.

"Grandma? What is it? Are you sick?" Izzy's voice was trembling. "Grandma?"

"She can't *talk*, Izzy! That's the universal sign for choking."

Izzy's grandmother nodded frantically and leaned more heavily against the counter.

"Quick, Izzy, do you remember what to do?"

"I . . . ah . . ." Izzy was beginning to panic.

"The Heimlich maneuver," Molly coached. "Your fist goes thumb-side in for an abdominal thrust."

Izzy reached for his grandmother and did as Molly said.

"Now administer an abdominal thrust."

Closing his eyes and gritting his teeth, Izzy did as he was told. His grandmother sagged weakly over his forearms.

"Again! It could take several thrusts before it works!" Molly's eyes were wide with fear, but her voice was steady. "And don't get too close to the rib cage or you could break her ribs."

Andrew drew a sharp hissing breath and sank into a chair, pale as a sheet and sweating.

But no one had time for Andrew. All attention was focused on Izzy and the frail, white-haired woman in his arms. Again, Izzy held his fist with his other hand and thrust backward sharply. Suddenly a large red and white peppermint shot out of the older woman's mouth, landed on the counter, and rolled innocently off the other side. The woman took a deep gulp of air and sank to the floor with her grandson's arms still around her.

Izzy was crying. Molly was crying. Sarah, Darby, and Jake were crying. Even Andrew had the threat of tears in his eyes.

"You saved my life, Isador. You saved it."

"Oh, Grandma, I was so scared. . . ."

"But you knew what to do, and you did it. I'm so proud of you. . . ." Tears streamed down her papery, wrinkled cheeks. "My grandson saved my life!" She reached for Izzy's cheeks and cradled them in her palms. "The Lord has blessed me, Isador." As naturally as breathing, Mrs. Mooney began to pray.

"Dear Heavenly Father, thank you for sparing my life and making my grandson Isador your instrument. Bless him and his friends and the project they are pursuing, for it is a worthy one."

"Ah, Grandma, don't do that." Izzy looked pleased and embarrassed as he helped her to her feet and guided her toward a chair.

"How did you know what to do, Izzy?"

"Molly, Sarah, and I learned about it at the class we attended. I was beginning to blank out. It's a good thing Molly was here to tell me what to do." His hand was trembling as he ran it through his hair. Though his grandmother seemed to be recovering, Izzy still looked shaken.

Darby didn't realize she was still crying until she felt a teardrop drip off the end of her chin and saw Jake catch it with the tip of his finger. No one seemed to know what to say.

Sarah broke the silence. "I think we saw a miracle tonight. If we hadn't gone to that class, none of us would have known how to help Izzy's grandmother."

"And that's the kind of miracle EMTs perform every day!" Molly's blue eyes brimmed with tears.

"Maybe we'd better save our work for another night," Jake suggested. "Izzy, get your grandmother settled. We'll clean up the living room."

Quietly they picked up their papers and straightened the pillows. Izzy joined them as they were about to leave.

"Grandma's lying down. She says she's fine. I want her to go to the doctor. Maybe Mom or Dad can convince her when they get home."

"You did good, Izz-man," Andrew said gruffly. "Really good."

They stood awkwardly in the doorway, reluctant to leave.

"Listen, guys, we've got to make this story great. I never realized until tonight how *important* the EMT program is. If I hadn't been in that class last night . . ." His voice trailed away. Everyone knew exactly what Izzy meant.

Sarah, Molly, and Darby left together with Jake and Andrew following close behind. All were quiet and shaken. Tonight they had been shown how thin the line between life and death could be.

"Are you awake?"

"Molly, it's only eight o'clock on a Saturday morning. Of course I'm not awake!" Darby scowled at her clock radio just as the digital face turned to 8:01.

"You have to come with me. I need your help."

"Doing what?"

"The makeover, of course! My appointments are today. I have to go in this morning to look at books and pick out my new hairstyle. I'm getting it cut at ten o'clock."

"Molly, you know what I think about this. . . ."

"You've *got* to come. Sarah is going with me, but you know how she is. She tells everyone they look nice. I need someone with me who'll be totally blunt. I'm considering a color change. How do you think I'd look with red hair?"

"Molly!" Darby swung her feet to the floor. "Pick me up in half an hour."

"Great. See you then."

———

"I'm getting nervous," Molly announced as Sarah drove toward the mall. "Gary is coming to Emmaline's

Salon at nine forty-five to do some 'before' shots. He's bringing Andrew along to teach him how to use the camera. If you don't think my hair would look good red, how about short—really short?"

"You look great now. It's fine if you want to get a facial and your nails done for the story, Molly, but you're crazy to think that a new hairdo will change Blake's mind."

Molly's hand stilled in the air as she was reaching to grab a stray curl. "Is that what you think I'm doing? Trying to get Blake back? Well, you're wrong. I don't even *want* him back. I just want to make him feel miserable, that's all. I just want him to be sorry he dumped me."

"For someone so little and petite, you sure have a thick skull," Darby muttered. "Forget Blake. Forget revenge. Look forward, not back."

"Here's the mall. Park in the red parking lot, Sarah; that's closest to the door we want."

Sarah sighed and did as she was told. There was to be no talking Molly out of her little escapade.

Emmaline herself was doing Molly's hair. She met Molly in the doorway to the salon, garbed in black tights, a baggy red and black sweater, and short-cropped hair dyed a deep burgundy.

"I'm so glad you're here!" Emmaline swooped down upon the girls. "Let's talk cut and color. Something dramatic, I suppose."

While Molly and Emmaline talked and flipped through mountains of books filled with hairstyles ranging from the garish to the sublime, Sarah and Darby twiddled their thumbs in the reception area.

"I think she's actually going to do it," Sarah murmured.

"Molly—as a redhead! She's going to hate it. Everyone will tease her, and Blake will probably be first in line to laugh." Darby glanced at Sarah's natural red hair. "No offense."

"It's not too late yet," Sarah said consolingly. "Maybe Gary can talk some sense into her."

"Oh, great! Now we're depending on a grown man with a ponytail and an earring to convince Molly to be more conservative?"

Sarah giggled. "I never thought of it quite that way. Let's go see how they're doing."

Molly was seated in Emmaline's chair with a plastic drape over her clothing. Emmaline was twiddling with Molly's curls.

"Your hair is rather stunning already, dear. Are you *sure* you want to do this?"

"Something dramatic. Older. Sophisticated. Curls aren't sophisticated."

"But they can be. Here, let me show you. . . ."

Before Emmaline had a chance to work her magic, Molly held up a hand. "I'm going to look better after you do this, aren't I?" Emmaline's comb paused over Molly's head.

"You'll look different."

"But better?"

Emmaline put down her comb. "Frankly, Molly, I can't promise. Sometimes, when people come in here for a change, a new look makes all the difference in the world. Other times . . . not."

"Why does it work for some people and not for others?"

"Because some people are trying to change things other than their hair."

"Huh?"

"If you're tired of your look and want to perk it up, a new hairstyle will do it. If you're tired of your *life*, it's going to take more than a cut or color to fix that."

Molly stared into the mirror with unblinking eyes. Neither Sarah nor Darby spoke. Molly put her hand on Emmaline's wrist. "Maybe I'm one of those people," Molly mused. "I'm changing my hair when the thing that needs changing is Blake's arrogant attitude!" Her jaw hardened. "Why should I try to do something for him when I should be doing what *I* want? I'm still letting Blake run my life, and he isn't even in it!"

"So what do *you* want? Black? A rich red? Short? Asymmetrical?"

Molly swallowed thickly and pulled at the drape around her neck. "I think something not quite so daring. I'm afraid I won't be comfortable. A trim might be nice or . . ."

"An excellent idea!" Emmaline dove happily into Molly's curls. "Frankly, I'd hate to see you do anything to this beautiful head of hair. Let's just do a deep conditioning treatment and then just stack it on your head with little loose curls cascading around your face. It will be marvelous for an 'after' photo and nothing you'll regret later."

"Sounds fine. You can start as soon as Gary's taken the 'before' photo."

When Emmaline excused herself to answer a phone call, Darby spun Molly around in the salon chair. "I'm so glad you changed your mind! What made you do it?"

Molly looked embarrassed. "I decided that I'm just

fine the way I am. If Blake Denton can't see that, why would I want him anyway? Besides, I'd look hideous with black hair!"

"Good for you!"

"Atta girl, Molly!"

They were all grinning when Gary arrived with cameras and Andrew in tow.

As Gary set up the shot, explaining each step to Andrew, Molly dragged her hair away from her face and put on her most glum expression. "How's this? No makeup, no expression. I've *got* to look better than this when I'm done, right? Look out, Blake! You're *still* going to be sorry you passed me by!"

———

Because the photo shoot was taking longer than expected, Sarah and Darby decided not to wait for Molly. Instead, they left her after Gary promised he'd give her a ride home.

"I hated to leave," Sarah said as she drove toward Darby's house, "but I promised I'd be home by noon."

"It's okay. Molly was living her modeling fantasy. She looked great, didn't she?"

"Absolutely. I'm so glad she didn't do something strange to her hair." Sarah smiled. "Frankly, I think that before Gary's done, those photos might make Blake a little sorry he was so quick to change girl friends after all."

"Andrew looked pretty interested in Molly, I noticed." Darby grinned slyly. "Maybe after today he'll have a new enthusiasm for working with our investigative team."

"What is it with Andrew, anyway?" Sarah asked, a frown creasing her forehead.

"What do you mean?"

"Why does he act the way he does? So . . . stuck on himself."

"Who knows? Maybe that's the way he was raised. His parents own Figaro's. Maybe he's used to being special."

Sarah whistled through her teeth. "Figaro's? Really? We ate there once. My dad said he bought his first car for less money than we spent on dinner. I didn't realize . . ."

"Andrew's used to being around people with money. Maybe he thinks he's so smart because no one's ever told him any differently."

"It's funny, isn't it?" Sarah mused. "On one hand, Andrew is too sure he's always right. On the other, Molly isn't nearly confident enough of herself. Too bad they can't trade a little self-confidence for a little humility. Then they'd both be perfect."

"Well, I think Molly's closer to reaching that than Andrew," Darby interjected.

"Yes, Molly finally realized it was her *feelings* that needed a makeover, not her face." Sarah smiled serenely. "I'd been praying that she'd figure that out."

Sarah laughed at the look on Darby's face. "I know, I know, it sounds weird, but I pray for a lot of things. If you get to know me better, you'll probably get used to it."

Would she ever get used to someone who prayed as easily as she talked to her friends? Darby settled back in her seat and watched the city go by. Time would tell.

CHAPTER 12

LIVE
FROM BRENTWOOD HIGH

"It's about time to do your laundry, Darby." Mrs. Ellison eyed the heaping mound of dirty clothes Darby had just deposited on the laundry room floor. "If all this is dirty, what have you been wearing the past two days?"

Darby ruefully studied her gray baggy sweats and tattered flannel shirt. "Dad's clothes mostly, but even he's running out."

"You've been awfully absorbed with this *Live! From Brentwood High* thing." Mrs. Ellison leaned against the utility sink and crossed her arms. "Are you sure it's not interfering with your other responsibilities?"

"You're sounding like a mother, Mom."

"What can I say? It's my job. I've never seen you so taken up with a project."

"I've never done anything like this before. It feels so ... important ... so *real*. I've always assumed that the life of a teenager is pretty responsibility-free. School, after-school jobs, friends, you know. But now, after meeting Grady and seeing what he does on the ambulance squad, it makes me realize that even at seventeen or eighteen I can make a difference in somebody's life!"

Mrs. Ellison put an arm around Darby's shoulder. "I can understand. I started to work as an aide in a nursing home when I was your age. Once I started working, I realized that even though I couldn't stop people's pain, I *could* make their existence more bearable. You're growing up, Darby."

"It's easier to be a kid."

Darby's mother chuckled and brushed a stray bit of dark hair away from her eyes. "When you were a kid, I did your laundry for you."

"I could stand to be a kid for a day...." Darby looked hopeful.

"I'll do the laundry if you'll cook meals to put in the freezer for the upcoming week. Lasagna, chicken and rice, meatloaf..."

"The laundry is sounding easier all the time." Darby was interrupted by the ringing phone. Her spirits brightened as she heard the voice on the other end of the line.

"Hi, Jake."

"What's up?"

"Not much. I'm doing my laundry. My closet is totally empty except for a winter coat and two ugly blouses that are too small anyway."

"Will you be done by tonight?"

Excitement butterflied in Darby's stomach. "I *could* be, I suppose. Why?"

"Just wondered if you wanted to do something—go out."

Jake is asking me for a date? Darby nearly dropped the phone into a box of laundry detergent.

"Just us? Not the *Live! From Brentwood High* people?"

"You *want* them along?"

"Not really. It would be great to go out with you, Jake."

"Good. I'll pick you up at seven. Dress casual."

"Okay. Sure. Thanks. 'Bye."

Darby gently hung up the phone and then, squealing, threw herself onto the heap of laundry on the floor. She lay there kicking her feet and yelling "Yes! Yes! Yes!"

"Good news, I presume?" Mrs. Ellison stuck her head into the doorway.

"Jake Saunders asked me out! Isn't that wonderful?"

"Haven't you been with him all week?"

"This is totally different. That was school. This is . . . *real!*"

"Did I miss the part about school not being reality?"

"Mom! Don't tease! He is *so cute* I can't stand it. I never really thought this would happen."

"And it won't if you don't get busy with this laundry."

Darby recognized the look in her mother's eye and jumped to her feet. In a moment she had the washer filling and the clothes sorted. Absolutely nothing was going to keep her from going out with Jake tonight.

———————

"Can you believe it, Sarah?" Darby had called her the moment she'd finished her chores.

"Chill, Darby. It's not like this is your first date ever, you know."

"But there's something special about Jake. He's older, more mature than most of the guys at school. He's cute. He's nice. He's considerate. He's . . ."

" . . . everything you could possibly want in a boyfriend?"

"Oh, Sarah! This is so *complicated*!"

"A second ago it was perfect. Why complicated?"

"It just occurred to me that if Jake and I are working together on *Live! From Brentwood High* we probably shouldn't be dating. If it doesn't work out—you know how difficult that could be."

"Aren't you being a little premature? He's asked you out *once*. Relax! Enjoy! Just make the decision not to get too serious—at least until *Live! From Brentwood High* is over."

"It really isn't a good idea to get involved with someone else in the program. Remember what Ms. Wright said about not looking for prom dates in these classes? This program is important to me, Sarah. I'd hate for anything to interfere with what I can do or learn. Maybe I should call Jake back and explain this to him. . . ."

"Haven't you heard of just having *fun*? Don't dream up trouble where there isn't any. You and Jake are mature people. You both realize that it's stupid to get tied down to a single person in high school. Tell him how you feel. He'll probably say he feels the same way."

"You're right. Jake and I can talk. Maybe I'm blowing this all out of proportion." Darby glanced at her watch. "I'd better get going. Mom won't let me leave till my chores are done. Gotta go, Sarah. Bye."

By the time the doorbell rang, Darby had completed her mother's "to do" list, hurried through a shower, dried her dark hair, and ruffled through the curls with her fingers. Though she normally didn't use much makeup, tonight she'd brushed a coat of mascara across her already long, dark lashes. A dusting of pale blush brought out the crest of her cheekbones.

Darby shrugged into a red denim jacket as she opened the door. "Hi."

"Hi, yourself. You look just right."

"For what?"

"For what we're going to do tonight."

"You look pretty 'right' yourself." Jake wore jeans and a gray-green sweater that matched the color of his eyes. His sandy hair had been tamed and feathered nicely above his ears. Darby's heart gave a little lurch.

"Come on, we have to hurry or we won't find a parking spot." Jake held out his hand. Darby's fingers felt small and warm tucked into his palm. She grinned and sighed and closed the door behind her.

They were quiet as they drove toward Jake's secret destination. The music from his tape player was loud and rhythmic.

"Nice car," Darby finally ventured. It felt odd to be shy around Jake, yet tonight she was.

"Thanks. I inherited it from my older sister. Took forever to get the perfume smells out of here."

"I didn't know you had an older sister."

"I have *four* of them."

"Really? What was that like?" It was hard for Darby, with only her older brother to contend with, to imagine such a family.

"You haven't lived until you've had four big sisters who thought you were their very own personal toy. They took me shopping, bought my clothes, made me be the baby when they played house, asked me my spelling words until I thought I'd go crazy.

"Then, when I got older, they started to give me advice about how to treat girls. I grew up sharing a bathroom with panty hose, hair dryers, curling irons, and scented bath soap. Neither Dad nor I ever owned a razor that somebody hadn't used to shave their legs.

"When I grew bigger than the girls, they started stealing my clothes. I don't have a shirt that hasn't been worn to a college class or on a date. They slept in my T-shirts, rolled the sleeves on my suitcoats and wore them as blazers, and made me take them places when they didn't have dates. *That's* what it was like!"

"Wow. I never imagined. Did you hate it?"

"Nah. It was great. My youngest big sister went to college last fall. I really miss her. The oldest just got married. I was a groomsman in the wedding. My wedding gift to her was that I didn't tell her new husband what she is *really* like. Poor guy is going to have to find *that* out for himself!"

Jake turned to grin at Darby, and deep, masculine dimples slashed his cheeks.

"No wonder you're so easy to be around."

"My mother says I'm 'broken in'—like a pair of old shoes. Nothing a female does can surprise me anymore. I've seen it all."

Darby relaxed against the leather-upholstered seat of the car. Those words were music to her ears. She and Jake were going to get along just fine. Those fears and concerns she'd expressed to Sarah seemed silly now.

"What are we doing tonight, anyway?" Darby asked as they traveled to the heart of Brentwood.

"Have you ever heard of the Brown Bag Concerts?"

Jake tipped his head for Darby to peek into the back. On the seat were two brown paper bags filled and folded neatly at the top. "Those are our tickets into the concert."

"But why?"

"Wait and see."

Jake parked the car, and after helping Darby out, he reached in the back for the brown bags and a blanket. In the distance Darby could hear an orchestra warming up.

"It's pops night," Jake explained. "A free concert. Besides bringing a brown bag supper to eat at the concert, we each have a can of food in our bags. That will be donated to the city's food pantry for the needy. We eat our supper, listen to the music, and the food pantry gets its shelves restocked. Neat idea, huh?"

Darby loved it. The park was already filling with couples carrying brown bags and blankets, just as she and Jake were doing. They found a comfortable spot on a little grassy knoll not far from the gazebo where the orchestra was set up. Jake spread out the blanket and flopped down. He held out a hand, inviting Darby to join him.

"Don't they worry about people messing up the grounds with their brown bag meals?" Darby wondered aloud.

"Not this group. Everybody's pretty conscious of the environment. My sisters started bringing me to these concerts when I was in junior high. Usually the park is as clean when we leave as it was when we arrived."

"I'm impressed," Darby admitted as the music began. Sarah was right. This was *fun*.

"By the way, what's for dinner?" She took the brown paper bag Jake offered and peeked inside. Flavored mineral water, cheese, crackers, and eclairs frosted with chocolate. "You packed this yourself?"

"Out of my sister's refrigerator. She says the quickest way to a girl's heart is chocolate. Is she right?"

"She is about this girl." Darby lifted out an eclair and ran her finger through the frosting.

They shared the food and the music as they watched the sky darken. The concert finished just as dusk was upon them. Then, from behind the gazebo came a shower of skyrockets bursting onto the night.

"How beautiful!" Darby gasped.

"You sure are."

She blinked but remained frozen where she was, staring at the night sky. Had she heard what she'd thought she'd heard? When she turned to him, he was staring at the fireworks display. Had she dreamed it? Had she *wished* the words into being? Darby didn't know.

They returned to the car hand in hand. Darby wore the blanket draped around her shoulders to ward off the chilly night air.

"Still cold?" Jake asked as they waited for their turn out of the parking lot.

"A little. But happy. That was the nicest evening I've spent in a long time."

"It's not over yet. Let's stop somewhere and get some hot chocolate."

"Sounds good to me." It was all Darby could do to keep from shivering. Nerves and the cold night air were playing havoc with her insides.

"I love Brentwood at night," Jake commented as they drove through the downtown district. "There's so much energy down here. People never seem to go to bed. My sister waited tables at a restaurant near here. She says people were still coming in for dinner reservations at eleven at night."

"After the theaters closed, I suppose. Mom and Dad took me to see *Romeo and Juliet* for my sixteenth birthday and then out for dessert."

"We saw it too. My sister Kathy's boyfriend had to work, so Kathy made me be her escort. It was great."

It was so easy to talk to Jake, Darby thought. They liked the same things. They shared similar opinions and attitudes. She ignored the uncertainties she'd experienced earlier. She'd worry about *Live! From Brentwood High* tomorrow. Tonight belonged to her and to Jake.

Jake turned into the parking lot of the Walters Family Restaurant not far from Brentwood High. "We might as well surprise Molly if she's working tonight."

"Good idea. Molly never seems very happy about her job. I don't think I'd like to work at something that made me that miserable. I suppose she doesn't have much choice."

Molly hurried to greet them after they'd been shown to a table. She looked attractive and serious in her brown and orange uniform. She even wore a tiny hat pinned into her curls.

"Don't say it," she said when she observed Darby looking at her hat. "I look like a milkmaid who should be running through the Alps, right? I hate these uniforms. They're dumpy, but Mr. Walters says we have to wear them. He's in the back room right now. I'd better take your order." She glanced over her shoulders. "If he thinks you're friends of mine and I'm visiting, he'll yell at me."

Darby was surprised by the miserable expression on Molly's face. She'd known that Molly worked two nights a week, but she'd assumed that Molly was *happy* to be working. Molly looked anything *but* happy tonight.

"Two hot chocolates."

"Is that all? Are you sure you don't want anything

to eat? Mr. Walters yells at us if we don't try to get the customers to order more food."

"Sounds like a nice guy."

"He's a total jerk," Molly hissed.

"How about two caramel rolls. Is that enough?"

Molly shot Jake a look of gratitude. "Fine. Thanks. I'll be right back."

She hurried off before anyone could say more.

"That was weird," Jake commented. "If I didn't know better, I'd say Molly was afraid of her boss."

"Maybe she is. She probably doesn't want to lose her job. Molly has to make all her own spending money. Her mom is divorced from her dad and remarried—for the second time. I don't think she gets much spending money from home."

"I didn't know that."

"Molly doesn't talk about it much, but I think that she's on her own, moneywise."

Jake whistled through his teeth. "I guess I'm pretty lucky. My parents have always given me an allowance for the chores I do around the house. And when I needed extra money, I could usually get it from one of my sisters."

"As a gift?"

"Are you kidding? No. I usually had to do something horrible to earn it—like clean their rooms or do their laundry. Once I had to walk my sister Jane's boyfriend's dog—a Doberman with an attitude. I'm lucky I came back alive."

"I like your sisters already—and I haven't even met them."

"Believe me, they're not so great in person—bossy, messy, noisy, snoopy."

"I'm liking them better and better!"

Jake and Darby were laughing when Molly brought their food to the table. It was Darby who first noticed that Molly's cheeks were flushed and her eyes teary.

"Something wrong?"

"Can't talk. Mr. Walters saw us. Act like you don't know me."

Obediently they took their food and avoided making eye contact with Molly. After she'd left their table, Jake frowned. "I don't think I like the way Molly gets treated here." They ate in silence, the invisible Mr. Walters becoming a mood-dampening presence.

When Molly returned with their bill, however, she was smiling. "It's okay now," she said. "He just left."

"Why do you work for such a crab?" Jake asked.

"The money. And it's okay most of the time—because he usually torments the day shift. But if someone gets on his bad side there's always big trouble."

"So stay on his *good* side."

A strange, wary expression flitted over Molly's features. "Sometimes that's dangerous too."

"What do you mean?"

"Never mind. Just forget I said that. Please?"

Because Molly looked so worried, both Jake and Darby nodded, not quite sure why they were agreeing.

"So where did you two go tonight?" Molly asked brightly, determined to change the subject.

Darby told her about the Brown Bag Concert in the park, about the fireworks, and about the cans people had brought to fill the city's food pantry.

"What a great story for *Live! From Brentwood High!*" Molly enthused. "It's good visually as well as being important to the community."

"You're right. We should tell Ms. Wright about it."

Jake groaned and slid a little lower in his seat.

"What's wrong with you?" Molly asked.

"Have you noticed that our whole lives are beginning to center on the *Live!* program? Everything we do or see is a potential story. I've started to plan my life around it."

"Me too. But think how much we've already learned!"

"I never realized that it would happen so fast. First, the birth of a baby, then getting to know Grady—and the thing with Izzy's grandmother . . . heavy-duty stuff."

"How is Mrs. Mooney doing?" Molly asked.

"Fine. Izzy said she had a sore throat for a couple days and that she's given up eating hard candy. Other than that, she's fine. It's *Izzy* who's changed."

"Izzy? What's that supposed to mean?"

"You haven't talked to him?"

"Not much lately. What's happening with him?"

"He's in this strange mood. He keeps talking about how his grandmother could have died if he hadn't gone to that class."

"That's not so surprising. It was a close call."

"Izzy's never faced death before. Now he acts like he's got to single-handedly do something about it."

"Well, I'll be facing death too if Mr. Walters comes back and catches me talking to you," Molly said, then headed for the kitchen. "I'd better get busy."

"Sorry if I brought you down with that conversation about Izzy," Jake said.

"It's okay. Izzy and I have been friends for a long time. I want to know if something is bothering him."

Jake slid his hand on top of Darby's. "Lucky Izzy."

CHAPTER **14**

LIVE

FROM BRENTWOOD HIGH

"Who's ready to tape their story?" Ms. Wright inquired. The *Live! From Brentwood High* meetings had taken on the atmosphere of a newsroom—casual yet filled with the electric energy of new ideas to explore. "Shane? Kate? Joshua? How about you?"

Joshua Willis shook his head. "Not yet, Ms. Wright. Our story isn't coming together like it should."

"Maybe you're expecting too much." Josh was known around school as a perfectionist. "In the world of television, a story happens, we write about it, put it on the air, and it's done very quickly. You'd never have this much time to put a news story together if you worked for a TV station."

"Maybe not for the nightly news, but if I were doing an investigative reporting piece, I'd be doing all the legwork each of the team is doing now, right?"

"Good point, Josh. I'm going to be very anxious to see your piece. But, in the meantime, we're allowing our expert cameraman to go to waste. Is anyone nearly ready for him?"

"We've got a lot done," Izzy offered for their team, "but I'm not sure we're ready to film yet."

"What's next on your agenda?"

"Grady is on call the next two nights. He arranged permission for us to follow the ambulance if it's called out. We're supposed to stay out of the way and not cause any problem for the rescue team.

"Who knows?" Izzy continued. "We might be sitting around for two days waiting for the phone to ring."

"I'll go with you," Gary Richmond offered. "Maybe we can get some good footage of the EMTs out on call. A visual of a moving ambulance, a flash of the expression on Grady's face . . . we'll get something. It's time to quit researching and start filming."

"Grady says most nights are quiet," Darby added. "Sometimes, though, they transport patients from the nursing home to the hospital."

"It's okay. I've got all night." As usual, Gary was dressed in soft, faded jeans and a nondescript jacket with many pockets and slots holding camera paraphernalia. He hadn't shaved for at least a week and his hair was pulled back into a ponytail. It was sometimes hard to believe he was an award-winning *anything*, but Ms. Wright had referred to his distinguished career often enough to convince everyone of its validity—and make everyone wonder what he was doing here, in a Brentwood high-school program, when he could be pursuing his career anywhere in the world.

Gary never seemed to sleep or to adhere to any schedule. His restless, nomadic lifestyle had been the topic of several discussions, but Richmond himself was still a mystery.

"Who's going tonight?" Gary asked. "Izzy?"

"I'm in." Izzy rubbed his hands together gleefully. "I hope we see some action."

"Molly?"

"Can't. I've got to work." Molly wrinkled her nose in distaste.

"Who else?"

"I can go," Darby volunteered, eager to see Gary in action.

"I wish I could." Jake closed his notebook and threaded his pen through the spiral binder. "But I promised one of my sisters that I'd pick her up for a class she's taking at the college. Her car is in the shop for repairs. We won't be back in time to get all the way up to Braddington."

Sarah shook her head when Gary looked at her. "Can't. I go to church on Wednesday nights. It's a family thing."

"That's okay." Gary swiveled around to face Andrew. "I guess that leaves you."

"Me?" Andrew's perpetual sneer turned into a scowl. "Why me?"

"Because I'd like at least three of you along. Everyone else has a good excuse. Do you?"

"Darby and Izzy are enough. I'd just be in the way."

"You'll be working. You won't be in the way. You're either part of this team or you're not. Which is it?"

Andrew fixed his eyes on Gary. "This is dumb. We're running around gathering information on a story that's going nowhere and is about nobody. So what if some kid in hicksville gets to ride around in an ambulance? Big deal. You're acting like I even care about this."

"Really. Tell me more." Gary's voice was deadly quiet, but Andrew didn't seem to notice.

"I can't see what good any of this will do. Somebody could just as easily interview this ambulance jockey in the parking lot of the hospital. You're making it harder than it has to be, that's all. Besides, I think this Grady is all talk and no show. You can't tell me that anyone would give a kid the kind of responsibility he says he has—not really. And even if he *did*—though it's unlikely—why would he *want* it? Now's the time to live a little, to goof off. Work comes soon enough anyway. The guy's a nut case if he's giving that up!"

Suddenly, and not of his own volition, Andrew was spun around in his chair. Izzy's big bearlike hands dug into Andrew's shoulders. "I'd just love to sit here and have a deep philosophical debate about that, Tremaine, but, frankly, I don't have time. You're coming with us. You haven't been pulling your weight, and it's time to start. Got it?"

Andrew's mouth worked, but nothing came out.

"I couldn't have said it better myself, Mr. Mooney." A grim smile marked Gary's features.

"Thank you, Mr. Richmond." Izzy's lips twitched in something between a smile and a grimace. He turned again to Andrew. "And since you'll be joining us whether you like it or not, you'd better just *like* it!"

Andrew looked like a pouty, spoiled child as Izzy loomed over him. If it had ever been possible to convince Andrew that some good could come of rural EMTs and of this story, it was past now.

———

Andrew was still sulking when Gary, Izzy, and Darby picked him up in Gary's car later that evening. He slunk out of his house, an impressive two-story colonial, to sit in the backseat of the car. He immediately crossed his arms defensively over his chest.

"Cheer up, Tremaine," Izzy coaxed. "This is going to be fun."

"Yeah, right. I suppose you enjoyed getting your wisdom teeth pulled too."

Izzy gave a toothy smile. "How'd you know?"

Little else was said as they drove through thinning city traffic into the country.

Darby was glad the ride wasn't any farther. Gary's car was at least ten years old and of questionable reliability. The floor was littered with bits of paper, gum and candy wrappers, along with stale popcorn. The car looked as disreputable and unkempt as its owner.

Still, there was something about Gary that Darby liked. Although she hadn't put her finger on it yet, she sensed in him a warmth and compassion that made her trust him and his judgment. Though she was nervous about what might transpire on ambulance call tonight, just knowing she was with Izzy and Gary made it easier.

"Is that him?" Gary pointed to a tall, slender boy washing a pickup truck.

"Hey, Grady!" Izzy hung out the window and bellowed at the top of his lungs. "What's up?"

Grady dropped the wet chamois he was holding and sauntered toward the car. "Not much." He patted the small black case attached to the waistband of his cutoffs. "I've got the beeper, but so far all is quiet."

"Are you absolutely sure this is all right?" Gary asked after introductions had been made. "Following the ambulance and all?"

"My supervisor said it was okay. He's eager to get our story out because he's as sold on our importance as I am. We're really making a difference in remote areas.

We're saving lives. Besides, the more volunteers we have, the fewer hours we have to spend on call.

"Unfortunately I can't promise that there will even *be* a call tonight. We're not like the city—with a large population dependent upon us. Calls are sporadic."

"We're patient," Gary assured him. "Any specific instructions for us should there be a call?"

"Just be sure to stay out of our way so that we can work, and don't do anything that will jeopardize the care and transport of a patient. Don't film the patients or reveal anything personal about them. Take as many pictures as you want of the ambulance and crew."

"What good is any of this if we can't take pictures of the people?" Andrew said, reminding them of his presence. "Do you actually plan to stand around here all night waiting for a call? You have to be nuts!"

Izzy gave a low growl and stalked toward Andrew. Only Darby's restraining hand and the sound of Grady's beeper kept him from bellowing a retort into Andrew's face.

"That's me," Grady muttered. "Catch up with me at the ambulance entrance to the hospital." With that, he jumped into the half-washed pickup and was gone.

CHAPTER **15**

LIVE
FROM BRENTWOOD HIGH

"Let's go. Izzy, you drive." Gary's voice galvanized them into action. By the time they reached the hospital, the ambulance was pulling away, red lights flashing. Gary, portable ENG camera on his shoulder, was already filming as the white and red ambulance veered out of the driveway.

The camera was one Gary had demonstrated in class. Scenes could either be recorded for future playback, as Gary was doing today, or signals could be sent via a microwave link for a live telecast. The camera was self-contained and automated so that when a cameraman was running after a news story, he didn't have to stop to do any setup maneuvers. As Darby watched Gary work, she could appreciate the camera's capabilities in unusual production situations.

Darby's heart caught in her throat. This was just like watching a story unfold on television—except this time she was there to watch it all.

Izzy was having a hard time keeping up. Gary, oblivious to the motion of the car on the road, kept the camera running. That left Darby and Andrew to stare at each other.

"What do you think has happened?" Darby asked

softly as she stared at the flashing red glow of the ambulance in front of them.

Andrew shrugged as if to indicate that whatever it was, it was hardly important enough to affect him. "Maybe a cow stepped on someone's foot. Or a farmer slammed his finger in the pigpen door."

"Stop it, Drew! This isn't funny."

"It is to me. Since I'm wasting my time I might as well laugh about it."

Darby only half believed him. Andrew looked pale beneath the normal duskiness of his complexion, and the skin around his lips looked pinched and tight.

"There it is!" Izzy shouted as he slowed the car behind a cluster of vehicles on the side of the road.

A single car lay on its roof in the ditch, as if it were an upside-down turtle flung onto its back. The roof had crumpled under the impact, and shattered glass sparkled like wicked diamonds in the grass. A girl about Darby's age lay on the ground in the spray of glass. A policeman already on the scene knelt beside her.

As Izzy pulled off the road out of the way of traffic, Gary flung open the door and hit the ground running, still filming.

"He certainly gets carried away," Andrew joked, betrayed by the tremble in his voice. Then even Andrew was silenced by the sight of another teenaged girl wandering aimlessly in the ditch, bleeding profusely from a head wound. Dazed and obviously confused, she occasionally lifted a hand to her eyes to wipe away the blood streaming into her face.

"Why doesn't someone help her?" Darby cried.

"Can we get any closer?" Izzy wondered.

"We mustn't interfere with the rescue team."

"Let's just get out of the car." Cautiously the three-some slipped from Gary's battered Chevy and stared at the flipped vehicle.

"Grady told me that being calm and professional are two of the most important qualities an EMT can have in the field. The victims must have confidence in an EMT's ability to help them. Besides, someone who's just been in an accident is probably disoriented—like that girl—and needs to be spoken to in a calm, slow voice."

Grady seemed to be doing just that. As they watched, he coaxed the young woman into sitting down and allowing him to begin a cursory examination.

"Patient assessment means 'listening, looking, and feeling' to determine what is going on with a patient. After he asks what happened and where the patient might hurt, he studies the general appearance of the patient."

"How does he know what to look for?"

"Skin color, sweating, blood. Grady said that you should be able to do an initial survey of the patient in sixty seconds or less. Then he checks for anything that might be life-threatening."

"What does that mean?"

"Making sure the patient can breathe and that there is no spine injury, bleeding, disorientation—all that stuff."

"I didn't know you knew all this, Izzy."

"I've called Grady a couple times just to talk. He's really an interesting guy."

No one had time to comment on Izzy's announcement because the EMTs began readying their patients for transport.

"They're good," Darby heard Andrew mutter under his breath as they watched the EMTs in action.

"Are you referring to the 'ambulance jockeys,' Andrew?" Izzy asked pointedly.

Andrew started to retort, but Darby interrupted him. "Check out Gary. It's as if he came alive once he started filming."

"I hope I get to try that," Izzy said as he watched Gary. "Hey! Something's going on! A second rescue team has arrived."

Now all activity seemed focused on the overturned vehicle. "Why is everyone running over to the car?"

"There's still someone in there!" Andrew gasped. "Why didn't they try to help that person first?"

"Triage, Andrew. Remember what Grady said? You'll be left until later if your injuries aren't life-threatening or . . ."

Andrew leaned heavily against the fender. "Do you think the person inside is . . ."

"Andrew? Are you all right?" There was a frantic, almost panicky look about him that alarmed Darby. "Do you need to sit down?"

Andrew grasped her forearm. "Somebody could be dead or dying in there. What if they can't get them out?"

"They're trained. . . ."

"You're shaking like a leaf, Andrew!"

"What are they doing now?" Andrew's feigned disinterest was gone. He stared fixedly at the overturned car and the men and women from the second rescue team working around it as they lifted a still body from the wreckage.

"Why is Grady's ambulance leaving? Don't they

have to help that guy they took out of the car?"

"Maybe the other team will take him . . . oh!" Izzy's voice trailed away as one of the rescue workers drew a sheet over the body lying on the ground.

"Maybe we should go now," Izzy said quietly. "Grady's gone. I'd like to catch him at the hospital."

"No!" The anxiety in Andrew's voice stopped them cold. "We can't leave yet! What about the guy on the ground? Why isn't anyone doing anything for him? They can't just leave him covered . . ." Andrew's protest ended in a ragged sob.

"There's no reason to hurry anymore, Andrew." Izzy spoke bluntly, stating the obvious. "He's dead."

"He can't be! He's just a kid."

"But old enough to drink and drive." Gary's voice startled them all. He thrust a microphone into Darby's hand. "Here, narrate what's been going on for the camera. We'll edit later."

"What should I say? Ms. Wright said we were supposed to have a script!"

"There are no scripts out here, Darby. Just talk. Tell the viewer what's happening. Put your heart into it." Darby saw the red light flicker to life on Gary's camera. He was filming.

Voice shaking, knees trembling, and visions of her most admired news reporters flooding her brain, Darby began. "This is Darby Ellison of Team One for *Live! From Brentwood High.* We're on the scene of a one-car rollover involving three Braddington teenagers. . . ."

Darby didn't even notice Andrew vomiting behind the fender of Gary's battered old car until Gary was done filming.

"Are you okay?" Darby leaned worriedly over Andrew as he slumped against the hood of the car.

"Yeah. Great. I always barf in public."

"I don't blame you. I felt like it too. If Gary hadn't made me take the microphone—"

"Stop it, Darby. Don't try to make me feel any better. I embarrassed myself, and nothing you can say will change that." Andrew's expression was bleak. His gaze drifted back toward the scene of the accident. "I've never seen a person die before."

"Come on, buddy." Gary put a gentle hand on Andrew's shoulder and guided him into the car.

Izzy and Darby sat in the backseat. Andrew slumped low in the front, saying nothing. Darby wasn't even sure Drew was awake.

Gary broke the silence as they drove back toward town. "Guess we got a little more than we bargained for, didn't we? Only good thing I can say is that it will make a powerful story. You kids got the scoop over every TV station around."

"Why doesn't that make me happy?" Izzy muttered miserably. "Great scoop. We have the footage of an accident scene in which a kid our age dies."

"Use it."

"Huh?"

"A tragedy has occurred. You saw it. Now what are you going to do about it? Seems to me that you can not only produce a story with real punch about teenagers who are making a difference and about the value of EMTs to rural areas but," Gary continued, "you've got some powerful footage to do a feature on drinking and driving. If I'd seen something like this at your age, it would have convinced me that alcohol and cars don't belong together."

"I guess I've always thought that, but it never seemed like a really big deal to me—until now." Izzy dropped his chin to his chest. "It always seemed like kind of a joke. Boy, was I wrong."

———

"Looks like Grady is back." Gary and the others watched as Grady's vehicle pulled into the driveway. Slowly, with the movements of an old, old man, Grady got out of his pickup truck.

"Guess you got your story," he said softly. "Sorry you had to wait so long for me to get back." He looked pale and shaken.

"We really didn't want a story like that one. We're sorry."

"Me too. The guy in that car was a high-school classmate of mine. The girls are a year or two younger. Good kids." Grady held out his hands. They were trembling. "Adrenalin. It's really pumping now. Sometimes I can't sleep after a call. I'm fine until I come home and then . . ."

"He was your *classmate*? But how could you . . ."

" . . . do my job? Because if I didn't, the girls could have died too." Grady shoved his hands into his pockets, but it didn't help. Even his shoulders were quivering. "Listen, I know you came out here to interview me, but if you don't mind, I think I need to be alone for a while."

"Are your parents home?" Gary asked.

"Yeah. I'll go talk to them. I'll be fine. And thanks for understanding."

Everyone was silent as Gary pulled out of the driveway.

"Are you all right?" Gary asked Andrew. "You look wasted."

"That kid was our age," Andrew said, as if Gary had never spoken. "That could have been me under that car."

"Or it could have been you on that rescue team," Gary pointed out bluntly. "Grady is your age too. We can't control everything that happens to us, but we can control our choices. Grady's chosen to do everything he can to save lives. The other boy chose to drink and drive. That's a risk no one *has* to take."

Andrew didn't answer. He slumped low in the seat again, his eyes fixed on the road ahead. Darby had never seen cocky, arrogant Andrew Tremaine so quiet.

It was a long, silent ride back to Brentwood.

CHAPTER **16**

LIVE

FROM BRENTWOOD HIGH

"You all right?" Gary eyed Andrew warily. "Maybe we'd better have some coffee before I drop you off. You look like something the dog dragged home."

"Thanks."

Gary grinned. "At least you can still talk." He pulled into the parking lot of the Walters Family Restaurant.

"Molly's probably still here," Darby said.

They trooped into the building just as Molly, wearing a jacket and carrying her book bag, was about to leave with Sarah.

"What are you guys doing here?" Molly demanded. "I thought you were going to see Grady."

Izzy took Molly by the arm and spun her around. "We're here for coffee. Join us."

"You don't have to be quite so caveman, Izz. I can follow directions." Molly stomped ahead, leading the way to a back booth.

"What are *you* doing here?" Darby inquired of Sarah.

"Molly asked me to give her a ride home when I was done with church. She knows I always have access to wheels." Sarah patted the wheel rim of her chair. "Get it? Wheels?"

Sarah waited until everyone else had climbed into the booth before maneuvering her chair up to the table. A waitress who was a little older than Molly took their orders—including the strong black coffee that Gary ordered for Andrew.

"Now then," Molly said as if conducting a meeting, "tell us everything about tonight. Did we miss anything exciting?"

No one spoke.

"*Something* must have happened!"

It was Andrew who spoke. "He died."

Molly's little bow of a mouth puckered. "Who died?"

"The kid the ambulance went to pick up. He was killed when his car rolled over. The two girls riding with him were hurt but alive. We followed them. We saw it all."

Both Molly and Sarah looked stunned.

Before anyone could say more, the story came pouring out of Andrew—the call, their trip to the accident site, the assessment and transport of the two passengers, the extrication of the driver—in graphic, emotional detail. He left nothing out, nothing to the imagination.

When they were at the accident site, Darby hadn't been sure exactly of how much Andrew was seeing or what he was thinking. She'd been so wrapped up in getting the story that she'd had no time to consider him. But he'd been there watching and, as was becoming fast apparent, taking it all in.

" . . . they just covered the body with a cloth . . ." he was saying. "He was our age." Andrew's voice lowered.

"I kept thinking that the guy should just get up and walk away. That's what happens on cartoons and in adventure movies. They walk away. But he couldn't." Andrew stared blankly into the cup of coffee the waitress had set before him. "This changes everything."

"What do you mean?" Gary put his arm across the back of the bench protectively, as if to shelter Andrew from his own emotions.

"It's just not fair! That's not supposed to happen to kids. They're not supposed to die."

"Who said so?" Gary asked. "Who made up the rule that kids can't get hurt or die?"

"Well, there's no rule like that really, I just thought . . ."

"Nothing has changed, Andrew. Nothing, that is, but you. You've realized for the first time that you're not invincible."

Andrew kept staring at his coffee, struggling to maintain his composure as Gary's words hit home.

"The rules haven't changed, Andrew. You were never as safe as you thought you were. But now you realize that you can't be careless or thoughtless or reckless because you *could* get hurt—or worse. Accidents have always happened. Now you know that they could happen to you too."

"I just remember seeing that kid lying there!" Andrew whispered. "In my mind I kept saying 'Get up! Get *up*!' I kept expecting him to stand up and start laughing. 'Hah! I fooled you!' he'd say. Then everybody would laugh and give him a rough time for tricking them and . . ." Andrew paused. "But he never got up."

"Growing pains," Gary said flatly. He gulped down his coffee and the cup clattered to the table. "Feels rotten, doesn't it? Growing up isn't much fun. I remember wanting to be old enough to get my driver's license. Then I wanted to be twenty-one so I'd be considered an 'adult.' When I turned twenty-one I assumed all my problems would be behind me." Gary's expression was more a grimace than a grin. "What a big fool I was."

Everyone was quiet. As though there was an unspoken agreement among them, Darby, Izzy, Andrew, Molly, and Sarah remained silent. It was the first time any of them had heard Gary speak in such personal terms.

"I grew up fast and hard, Andrew. I've seen so many things that shouldn't have happened that I don't think any of us are safe anymore. The Gulf War. Bosnia. Somalia. I covered them all. People dying in the streets. Bullet wounds. Starvation. Mass murder. I've seen more people die in a day than most people could even imagine. I've had my camera running in hospitals. I've filmed little children who were alive one minute and dead the next. I've seen people drinking filthy water from a pit in the ground. I've seen men die in their wives' arms and flies crawling in the eyes of dying babies.

"And I've had to keep my camera running because it's my job. Sometimes I've wanted to sit down and weep but I couldn't. It wasn't my job to cry."

"Is that why you quit, Gary?" Sarah's question was gentle.

He looked startled, as if he'd forgotten any of them were there. "I guess it is. I needed a break. I wanted to be away from death and destruction and misery. So, when Rosie Wright called me and said that there was a job for me here in Brentwood working with high-school students, I came. I thought I could get away from some of the pain I'd seen, but the pain is still here, only in smaller doses."

Sarah was tucked close to the table in her wheelchair, leaning forward intently, her startling eyes on Gary and Andrew. "I don't believe the world is all that bad. Bad things happen in this world, but good things happen too. Perhaps right now all you can think of is the negative, but life also has a positive side."

"You can say that?" Andrew asked. "From a wheelchair? If anyone thinks the world is a crummy, unfair place to live, it should be you!"

"I was more fortunate than the boy you saw tonight. He's dead. I'm not."

Andrew stared at Sarah and her chair as if seeing them both for the first time. "It must be a little like dying though, isn't it?"

"It's a *lot* like it!" Sarah said. "At first I thought I got the raw end of the deal. Some days I would have considered death the 'lucky' way out, but not now. Not anymore."

"What changed?"

"I realized that I'm more than just a pair of legs. I can't walk, but I can sing, read, write, laugh, have friends, be a friend. I can do and be lots of things that don't require legs. I don't want to give everything else up because one part of me was taken away."

"It doesn't seem fair," Andrew said softly. "You shouldn't have had to suffer like that."

Izzy and Darby exchanged a look punctuated by raised eyebrows and startled expressions. Neither had ever considered Andrew the compassionate type.

"Why?" Sarah asked quietly. "Who says kids can't get hurt?"

"It's not that they *can't*, exactly," Andrew stammered, "but they *shouldn't*. There's too many things left to do and to see. Illness and injury should be for *old* people!"

"Hey! Get it into your head: It's not true," Gary barked. "That's why kids get sexually transmitted diseases. That's why they total their cars and are surprised to wake up paralyzed."

"Thanks, Gary. That's a real downer."

"Yeah. This conversation is making me depressed!" Molly declared.

"When my grandfather died, it didn't seem so bad," Andrew said softly. "He'd been sick a long time. I'd never known him when he was well. It seemed okay for him to die—like the time was right. But it just doesn't seem right that a guy my own age should . . ." Andrew looked up, an intent expression marking his features. "Where do you go when you die?"

No one spoke. Instead, they all looked at one another uneasily, as if each had an *idea* but no one was confident enough to express it.

"I don't know," Molly said honestly. "I wish I did."

"Heaven. I believe you go to Heaven." Sarah was confident in her answer. "I thought about it a lot when I was in the hospital. I wondered what would have become of me if I'd lost more than the use of my legs. I tried to imagine what it would be like to die."

She put her hand on Andrew's. "Strange as this might sound to you, I wasn't afraid. I experienced a . . . peace . . . that I couldn't explain. That was the first time I realized for myself that there *is* a God. He was there with me, in the hospital, helping me get through all the things I couldn't have without Him."

"This sounds spooky," Molly blurted.

"It probably does, but it's not really. And I don't mean to give you a sermon, but I want you to know that there is Someone watching out for us. You might disagree, but that doesn't change the fact that He's there. I know it. I've met Him—up close and personal."

"Eeewww!" Molly shuddered. "I don't like this conversation! I don't want to think about dying. I want to think about *living*! I wish you'd never gone to see Grady."

"I'm glad you did." Gary's expression was thoughtful. "I've never thought about life or death all that much, because most of my life I actually didn't care whether I lived or died. I'd cover a war and wonder 'Why them? Why not me?' I began to feel very small and insignificant. You guys have made me think."

"Have we answered any of your questions?" Izzy had created a stack of bent straws and crumpled napkins in front of himself, signs that though he hadn't had much to say, he'd been listening intently.

"Not a one."

"Why is it that every good conversation brings up more questions than it answers?" Izzy growled.

"Enough heavy stuff!" Sarah shoved herself away from the table. "We all need time to absorb what we've talked about, don't you think?"

"Think, think, think. That's all I've had to do lately," Molly moaned. "I'm going to have callouses on my brain!"

"Then at least there will be *something* between your ears!" Izzy retorted.

The laughter was a welcome relief. Everyone had become pretty intense. Darby stared admiringly at Sarah. There were things she could learn from the girl in the wheelchair.

"Oh, yuk!" Molly muttered, breaking Darby's train of thought. "Here *he* comes."

"He" was Mr. Walters, Molly's boss.

Mr. Walters drew Molly aside, talking quickly, his face very close to hers. Darby could see discomfort on her friend's features. When Walters put a controlling hand on Molly's shoulder, Molly shrank back; still Walters' possessive grip remained where it was.

"He's kind of a sleaze-bag, isn't he?" Andrew commented. "I wonder why Molly puts up with him."

"Money. They pay well here and the tips are great. Nobody ever quits, so it's hard to get on staff."

Gary also followed the exchange between Molly and her boss.

When Molly finally broke away, Gary reached out and took her arm. "What's going on?" He was careful to sound casual.

"Trust me," Molly said in a tone so breezy it almost hid the quiver in her voice. "You don't want to know."

"Your questions look great, Darby. I like the idea of doing a semiscripted show. Your team has done a super job." Ms. Wright, dressed in billowing harem pants, sandals, and a blazer, strode across the television studio, waving Darby's notes in her hand during a break in taping. "What's next?"

"We're doing the final interview for the rural EMT story here. Grady wanted to see our studio."

Darby had decided on a semiscripted show—one in which the dialogue was not completely written out—because it would give her and Grady the opportunity for more give and take during the interview. She'd already scripted her opening and closing remarks and indicated for the director—Izzy—when to roll the videotape of the footage Gary had filmed at the accident scene.

The interview would be seen live in several classrooms and taped for replay later at strategically placed TV monitors in the hallways. An edited version would play on the local cable station during the ten o'clock news.

To hide her nervousness, Darby glanced around the television studio. She looked up at the array of spotlights and floodlights suspended from battens near the ceiling and then down to the impressive and complex-looking studio cameras sitting like hulking giants on the pneumatic pedestals that made it possible to maneuver them.

"Do you think Grady will like it?"

"What's not to like? It's a great studio." With a wave of her hand, Ms. Wright took in the lights suspended from the ceiling, the cameras, and the centerpiece of the room: the news desk, or as Ms. Wright and Gary referred to it, the "news set."

It was just like the ones on the national nightly news, the performance area of the newsroom where a person might see Peter Jennings or, in this case, Darby Ellison, reporting the news.

Live! From Brentwood High was emblazoned in blue across the beige wall behind the desk. No matter how many times she crept into the studio to look at the set, Darby never lost the thrill of seeing it—so professional, so *real*. When she was in the studio it was as if she knew this was the place she belonged.

"You love it here, don't you?" Ms. Wright's voice was soft and gently amused.

"It shows?"

"Like a beacon. I've seen others who can't get enough of the energy, excitement, and hard work that goes with putting together a show. You're a natural for this business. I can tell."

"Then why do I feel so nervous right now?"

"Because you are about to do your first on-air interview. It's perfectly natural." Ms. Wright tilted her head. "I hear a lot of commotion outside. I think your guest has arrived."

Darby entered the control room to find Grady surrounded by the members of Team One. Izzy was acting as director today and Molly as assistant director.

"What's going on?" Grady tipped his head toward the studio, where Andrew and Sarah were seated behind the news desk.

"They're taping the news. We take turns being anchors, camera people, everything. They'll be finished soon."

"What's that guy doing?" Grady asked. He pointed to Josh Willis, who stood behind one of the two large studio cameras.

"He's the floor manager, the link between the anchors and the director. He's the one who communicates with the performers while they're on the air."

"How does he do that?"

At that moment, Josh cupped his hands behind his ears. Immediately Sarah began to speak up.

"See that? She was talking too softly, so Josh gave her a directional cue to speak more loudly."

"How'd she know what he meant?"

"We've gone over the cues in advance. Josh can tell us if we're speaking too slowly or quickly, how much time is left in the segment, or even how to hold up an object so it can be picked up on camera. We aren't very good at it yet, but we'll get better with practice.

"Ms. Wright says that the sign of a good performer is that he or she reacts immediately and smoothly to all cues. Better yet, a professional shouldn't even *need* cues."

Darby looked at Grady. "Now that I've made you really nervous, should we get this show on the road?"

"Today we are interviewing Grady O'Brien, an eighteen-year-old high-school senior from Braddington, located thirty miles north of Brentwood. Grady is a part of the emergency medical rescue team which is credited with saving the lives of dozens of Braddington residents.

"Tell me, Grady, what has been your most rewarding rescue to date. . . ."

Darby was startled to see Josh signaling her for a wrap.

Grady seemed equally surprised. "Over already? That wasn't so bad." He ran a finger around the collar of his shirt to relieve the pressure.

"You can take the tie off now. We're done. I think it went pretty well." Darby stuck a pencil behind her ear. "Now all that's left is to talk to the kids who were watching and get our reviews." She glanced at the commotion still occurring in the control room. "But that can wait a bit."

She leaned back in her chair and studied Grady's face. "Do you mind if I ask you another question?"

"You're full of them, aren't you?"

"I guess news reporting is in my blood." She looked at him intently. "How are you handling the accident we saw?"

"All right. One day at a time. My supervisor says that in order to deal with what he sees and does, he builds a little shell around his emotions, a protective cover to hold them in so that they don't boil out and prevent him from doing the best job that he can. It sounds pretty cruel and callous at first, but I think he's right. I used to wonder how he could remain so calm and collected. Now I know it's because his shell—his protection—has had longer to develop than mine."

"And you *want* that to happen?"

"I *need* to have it happen. I have to stay strong so that I can do the very best possible job." He leaned back in his chair, and a wistful expression passed over his features. "The other thing I've learned is that life has no guarantees."

Darby and Grady were quiet, unaware of the hubbub around them. Darby felt a growing sense of loss. Grady had stepped into adulthood. Doing this story had drawn her along the same path. Was this what growing up was all about?

———

On Saturday night Team One, along with Grady, Josh Willis, Shane Donahue, Kate Akima, and Julie Osborn, were gathered around the large screen television in Jake Saunders' basement.

Izzy and Molly were dispensing popcorn and orders while the rest jockeyed for seating space directly in front of the TV. Only Shane Donahue sat off to the side by himself. It had surprised them all when he'd shown up at Jake's door. Though he'd been invited to watch the premier of the first *Live! From Brentwood High* story on the local Saturday night news, no one had expected him to actually come.

"Here it is, here it is!" Molly squealed. She dived into the mass of bodies and dug herself a place.

"Get your foot out of my ear, Ashton," Andrew complained.

"Do you always behave like this?" Julie sniped. "I'm glad we weren't on your team for this project."

"Shhhh. Here's our story."

They were all silent as Darby's face flickered onto the screen.

When it was over, and Darby's image had faded to black, Izzy raised his hand into the air for a high five. "Awright!" Molly put two fingers between her teeth and gave an eardrum-piercing whistle. Even the usually reserved Kate drummed her heels against the floor.

The nervous knot in Darby's midsection began to slowly unravel.

"What did you think, Darby?" Jake's face was close to her own, and she could see the fine smile lines radiating out from the corners of his eyes and barely crooked tooth that gave his smile so much charm. Her heart gave an involuntary lurch.

"Good. Fine. Okay."

"*Okay?*" Grady blurted. "It was terrific. You were stupendous on camera. Gary's camera work was phenomenal. Even if I'd never heard of EMTs before, I'd still want to sign up for the program!"

"Really, Grady, do you mean it?"

"Sure. Frankly, I wasn't all that confident that you guys could pull it off. The EMT program means so much to me, it was a little scary to share it with a group of . . ."

"Amateurs?" Jake provided the word with a smile.

Grady blushed. "Yeah. But you did a great job, a professional job. Thanks."

"Let's celebrate!" Izzy jumped to his feet with surprising grace for one so large. He flipped on the CD player and filled the room with music.

The others joined him laughing and talking. Kate, Julie, and Shane stood apart, discussing their own project. Only Darby sat back. She stared at her new friends and was filled with surprising feelings of affection. They hadn't been together long, but already they had shared things that made their connections run deep.

And, as new ideas for *Live! From Brentwood High* began to creep into her mind, Darby realized this was only the beginning. . . .

———

Something is very wrong with Molly's after-school job. Will it take the entire *Live! From Brentwood High* staff to expose her terrible secret? Find out in *Price of Silence*, Book #2 in the *Live! From Brentwood High* series by Judy Baer.

A Note From Judy

I'm glad you're reading *Live! From Brentwood High.* I hope I've given you something to think about as well as a story to entertain you. If you feel you have any of the problems that Darby and her friends experience, I encourage you to talk with your parents, a pastor, or a trusted adult friend. There are many people who care about you!

I love to hear from my readers, so if you'd like to receive my newsletter and a bookmark, please send a self-addressed, stamped envelope to:

> Judy Baer
> Bethany House Publishers
> 11300 Hampshire Avenue South
> Minneapolis, MN 55438